Treasured Tales

Edited By Briony Kearney

First published in Great Britain in 2023 by:

Young Writers
Remus House
Coltsfoot Drive
Peterborough
PE2 9BF
Telephone: 01733 890066
Website: www.youngwriters.co.uk

Book Design by Ashley Janson

Softback ISBN 978-1-80459-484-1

Printed and bound in the UK by BookPrintingUK
Website: www.bookprintinguk.com
YB0539R

Foreword

Welcome reader, come on in and enter a world of imagination!

This book is jam-packed full of stories on a whole host of topics. The Magic Door was designed as an introduction to creative writing and to promote an enjoyment of reading and writing from an early age.

A simple, fun activity of imagining a door and what might lie on the other side gave even the youngest and most reluctant writers the chance to become interested in literacy, giving them the key to unlock their creativity! Pupils could write a descriptive piece about what lay beyond their door or a complete adventure, allowing older children to let their ideas flow as much as they liked, encouraging the use of imagination and descriptive language.

We live and breathe creativity here at Young Writers – it gives us life! We want to pass our love of the written word onto the next generation and what better way to do that than to celebrate their writing by publishing it in a book!

Each awesome author in this book should be super proud of themselves, and now they've got proof of their imagination and their ideas when they first started creative writing to look back on in years to come!

There is nothing like the imagination of children, and this is reflected in the adventures in this anthology. I hope you'll enjoy reading their first stories as much as we have.

Contents

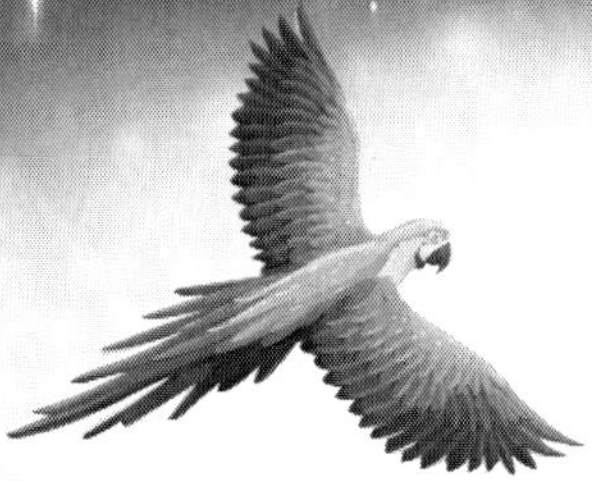

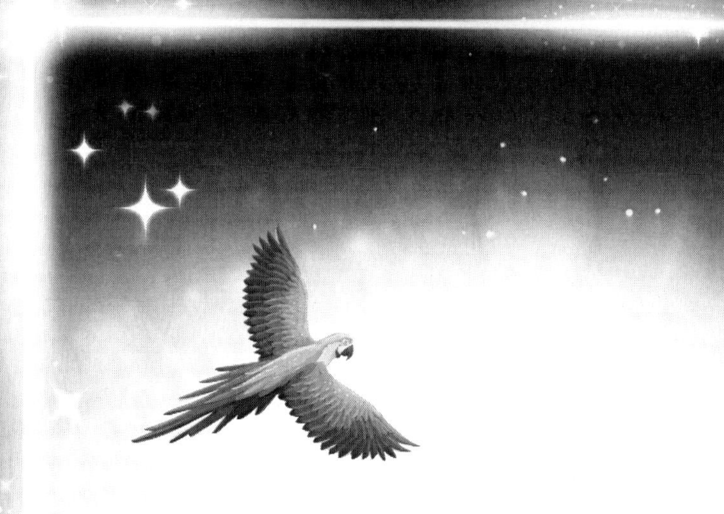

The Stories

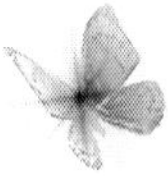

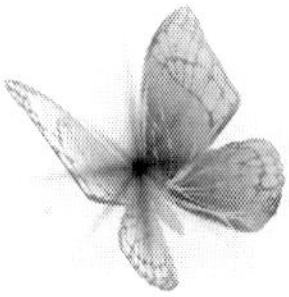

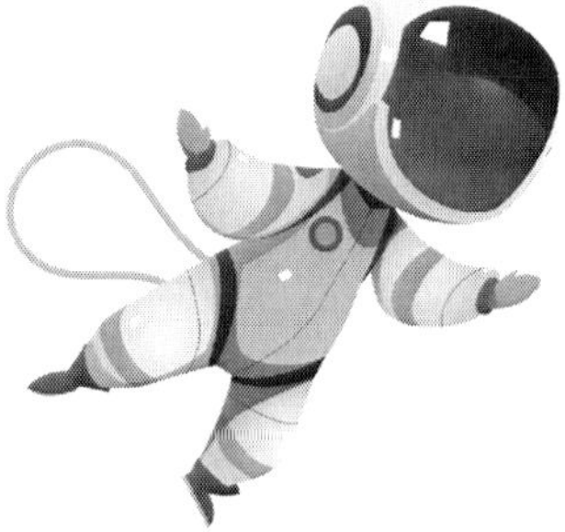

The Mystery Door

When I went to forest school, I heard a weird, twinkling sound. I began to walk, walking as fast as I could when I heard whispering in the distance. As I continued, I heard someone shouting behind me. "Alisha! Where are you?" the voice said.
I started to run as fast as I could, my heart was pounding. *Wait!* I thought. *Look behind you*. I saw the best door I'd ever seen in my life. I couldn't believe my eyes. There was a huge map underneath me. Then, "*Boo!*" I jumped when I heard that sound. There was a girl. Not a girl, but a ghost. She said hi and I was going to say hi too but I got sucked into a black hole.
I felt like I was going to faint. Before I knew it, I was upside-down. I tore the rope I was tied to and I fell. I fell and I landed in another door. I realised I was in the story of Little Red Riding Hood! As I walked along a path, I felt something behind me... a wolf! I was pinned to the ground by a wolf!

Alisha Tambuza (8)
Berger Primary School, Homerton

Mystery Milky Way

An extract

My heart was in my mouth. This couldn't be happening to me! I felt as though I was inside one of my dreams from when I was little. There, before me, was a door to an outer space galaxy. It was a platinum door with purple writing saying, *This is your dream world*. It had some rainbow rings, a bit like Saturn's rings, and there were also some rainbow ribbons.

I was standing there, a bit frantic but still excited. It had a beautiful glowing red beside it. I went up the blue steps and, just as I touched the ancient handle, I stopped dead. On the handle was a language. I stopped because I felt as if I'd seen it before. Yes! It was my friend, Asmin trying to trick me. It said, 'Haha! You'll never get through!' *Yes, I will*, I thought.

I opened the door and there she was, astonished.

"How in the world did you get here?" she shouted.

"Suppose you left the door unlocked," I said.

"Darn that lock!" she said with anger.

"What's up, Asmin?" I asked.

"Down on Neptune, Sammy was caught," she said angrily.
"Oh no, but who's Sammy?"
"An alien!" she said. "I'm not lying. An actual alien, I swear."
She looked worried so I tried to cheer her up but the truth was, I was worried too. We kept banging on the door but it didn't work. Well, there was nothing wrong with exploring!

Edna Zekarias (9)
Berger Primary School, Homerton

The Magic Door

When I walked through the door in the deep, dark forest, all I could see was another forest. But this forest had magic! Fairies flew, mushroom-people greeted people and, of course, there was the King and his knights. But then everyone looked at me with eyes and mouths wide open.
"Uhh, what's going on?" I said, startled.
The King came out. He looked like an elf, but really chubby. "Oh my, we haven't had a human for so long," said the King, giving me some food and coins. "Please, make yourself comfortable," said the King happily.
"Okay, thank you, but I should get going," I said tiredly.
"Don't go! We will tell you everything," the King shouted quickly.
"Fine, tell me, please," I said, wanting to go home eagerly.
"Basically, we want you to stay because we think you're powerful. We look up to humans as our gods."
"Well, that's completely wrong," I said, half asleep.
"She doesn't look like a god." A little elf appeared out of nowhere.

"I suppose you're right. Look at her." A mushroom-person appeared.
More people started to say this, and the King said, "Enough! I suppose you aren't a god. Let her out."
Then I woke up. All of that was a dream so I went back to sleep, hoping I could have another dream like that.

Margo Gascoigne (9)
Berger Primary School, Homerton

The Land Of Magic

An extract

The door was old and mysterious. When I opened it, there was a flash of blinding light and I was in a magical land. Everywhere I looked there were elves. Singing in the street, dancing to harp music, and entering gleaming crystal buildings. In the air, there was a magical tingle and hum that seemed to be in everything. I suddenly realised that I was feeling the magic!

As I walked down the cobbled streets, elves stopped to stare at me and then I could see they had sharp pointy ears. All of a sudden, I felt a strange sensation on my back and I was lifted into the sky! It was the most wonderful feeling.

"Hey! Over here!" whispered a high, sweet voice. I turned around in mid-air and saw another elf about my age. "Hi," she said again.

"Hello, what's your name?" I asked.

"I'm Raya, where did you come from?" she questioned.

"I came from London. I came here through a magical door," I answered. "Oh, and my name is Sylvie."

"Why don't I show you around and then you can go back home?" she said.
"Sure," I replied.
Raya led me all over, showing me the incredible wonders of the hidden world. We flew some more and I saw a diamond palace, a pink ocean, and a sidewards growing garden. Raya guided me back to the door. I was sorry to leave her behind.

Sylvie Einhorn (9)
Berger Primary School, Homerton

The Magic Door

As I walked down the dark, damp alleyway, I heard a strange noise that I thought I'd heard before but couldn't seem to recognise. I walked closer to the noise, feeling eerie inside. The majestic noise got louder and louder, a song from my childhood.
I saw a mysterious glow. I walked toward it, listening to my gut, risking my life for a... giant, vibrant door. It had a massive lock. I needed a key to open it. I found the key behind a tree and unlocked the door. My vision turned pitch-black for a millisecond. Not knowing what'd just happened, I realised I was in a fairy land!
It was filled with waterfalls, kind fairies and pixies, one of the friendliest giants ever, free cotton candy, and everything! Beautiful nightingales sang and played the harp. A jaw-dropping and mouthwatering experience. This couldn't be happening. It had to be a dream. But it wasn't! All my friends were there, it was absolutely incredible. After some time, it was dinnertime. I was so happy because they let me eat dessert first! The dessert was fairy cotton candy cake mixed with bubblegum and sprinkles. For the main meal, I could ask for anything and I would get it in under a minute!

I thought it was time to leave, but they said I could stay, even my family and friends. It was amazing but I knew I had to go back to the real world.

Lina Kherfi (9)
Berger Primary School, Homerton

The Magic Door

My heart was in my mouth. This couldn't be happening to me! I felt as though I was inside one of the stories I used to read when I was little. There, before me, was a magic door. The door was covered in vines of all types of green. It gave me an eerie vibe. I touched the golden handle and I felt an indent on it. It was fairies dancing majestically engraved on it. Could this be true? Fairies existed?

I moved the vines out of the way and pushed the squeaky door open. I saw fairies! They were floating everywhere. I also saw something scary: giant ants! I avoided the ants and went to speak to a fairy. "Hello, may I ask where I am?" I said calmly.

She said, "Well, you are in the world of fairies. Did you come through a door with magical vines?"

"Yes, but I didn't know they were magical!" I said, surprised.

"Yeah, they're covered in fairy dust. If a person touches them, they become the fairy that must find the crystal. It can transform a person into a fairy if they want."

I walked down into the depths of the fairy world where the crystal was. It was very dark and gloomy. There was a door with tiny cracks. Inside the cracks, I saw the crystal! I found it! I returned it to the fairies. They said I could stay but I said, "No, I need to go back."

Zaina Ullah (9)
Berger Primary School, Homerton

A Simple Show, Or Was It?

I loved magic ever since I was a little girl. My parents decided to take us to a magic show. I watched in fascination until the end of the show. There was a white, glowing spot backstage and it looked like a fallen star from far away. I gathered my friends and started to search.
We walked up to the scene and saw the glowing spot but, in fact, it wasn't a spot at all. It was a box with a button on it of a door. We pressed it together. Suddenly, we found ourselves teleported in front of a neon green door. We went in.
"Wow!" I said with my mouth wide open. We were in a world with animals, waterfalls, rainforests, and a cottage. There were paths and stepping stones, bushy trees and bamboo. There was nothing better than taking walks in this world. It was so refreshing.
Soon, night was approaching. We settled in the white cottage. It turned out to be very comfortable.

When we woke up, we searched around the house for a way back home. Finally, we saw the same button. We pressed it and found ourselves back at the show. We were relieved.

Miray Onel (9)
Berger Primary School, Homerton

The World Of Pokémon

I walked to a door on a colossal island and approached it carefully. It had some creature markings on it. Some of the markings were big and some were small. I reached for the handle and turned it. The door opened.
I peered through and saw what I'd dreamed about - it was Pokémon! I dashed through the door before it closed. When I went through the door, I realised I didn't have any Pokéballs. But I knew Professor Cerise had some so I went there and got a Pokéball and caught my first Pokémon! It was a Dragonite.
I battled with Dragonite and caught a Groudon. I decided to go on a catching spree and caught legendary Pokémon like Raquaza, Rapidash, Celebi, Zapdos, and Tapu. I kept on battling until I was the best trainer ever. Then, I went to the Galar region and caught Pokémon there. That was how I became the best trainer ever.

Malakai Franco Adjei (8)
Berger Primary School, Homerton

The World Of Pokémon

As I walk in, I see the island, volcanoes, and ocean.
It is shaded by palm trees. I smell fruit as I pass by.
I feel sand dunes that make me dizzier and dizzier.
I see different markings across the island. I hear birds chirping, leaves rustling, the wind blowing gently. No one is here except creatures.
It isn't noisy, like school, but coconuts are falling around me. It's a tornado coming! I go to a hot, steaming place. A volcano. I see Malakai. I can't believe it. He is trapped and the volcano is erupting! I get some knives to cut the rope and safely we make it out.
We are back on the shore and then, in front of us are 31 Pokéballs. We catch lots of Pokémon but we stop and see a Charizard and a Raichu. High above is a Dragonite. We catch them all in one go.

Kevin Duy Ung (8)
Berger Primary School, Homerton

The Snow Globe Of Wonder

One winter day, I was walking through the forest and found a door. As I opened the door, I was inside a winter wonderland snow globe!
Unexpectedly, a talking Arctic fox came to me and said, "Hi," in a confused voice. After a while, me and the Arctic fox went to explore and saw gingerbread houses and other talking animals. We could also see glittering and gleaming snow.
As we went past all the animals and gingerbread houses, we could hear shrieks, yelps, sighs, howls, and growls. After a while, we were still walking and could feel the soft glittering snow and the wind blowing in our faces. We also felt calm but cold.
Before long, me and the Arctic fox passed a giant hot tub filled with hot chocolate. In the distance, we could also see more gingerbread houses. As quick as we could, we went to get hot chocolate.
All of a sudden, a snowboarder came and said, "Hi!" Then he left.
"Oh, what a great adventure," I sighed in sadness.

In the morning, I woke up in my room and thought all of it was a dream. Oh, how I wished the adventure didn't end!

Izzy Collings (9)
Broadway First School, Broadway

The Crystals In The Magic Door

Once a week, a strange door always opened when the school bell rang. When the children ran to play, Elanor, Lara, and I peeked in. It was like a tunnel that went smaller and smaller. We walked in, then we had to crawl on the damp floor. Centipedes crawled on our spines as rats' eyes glowed red.
Squeak! Squeak! "What's that?" said Lara.
"I'm not sure," whispered Elanor.
Squeak! Squeak! Big red eyes opened and soon it wasn't dark. It was a dragon! It was a door with crystals. They opened and closed right in front of us. We crept in. One foot, then two feet, then three feet in.
"Wow!" Elanor said. Lara gasped as dragons flew across a purple sky. In the distance, massive crystals glowed. The door closed behind me and we ran to the massive crystals glowing. There were caves and ditches.
Boom! "Lightning!" Elanor yelled.
"Ssh!" Lara quickly whispered.
There was a sleeping dragon. But it wasn't any old dragon, it was a crystal dragon!

We tiptoed past and there were the crystals glowing. We looked away... but Lara wasn't there. She'd gone back to school.
"There! The door in the playground!" Me and Elanor ran to the door.

Elana Myatt (10)
Crossroads Primary School, Dunnet

The Two Doors

I was walking in a dark and gloomy forest.
Suddenly, a beam of light appeared and it lit up two doors. One door had holes in it and the other one was an old oak door.
I opened the door with holes in it, then I crept in and saw men, lots of men. The men had guns. All I could hear was gunfire. One soldier came toward me and yelled, "Get out!" I ran to the door, then I opened it and went back.
I opened the other door and peeked in. I saw a castle on top of a hill and then saw a dragon. I ran to the castle, then the dragon saw me! I quickly opened the doors and went up some steps. At the top of the castle was a princess and she cried, "Please get me out of here! Please!"
I said, "Okay!" then we ran outside. I ran to the door, the princess ran home. I opened the door and ran inside.

Dylan Macdonald (10)
Crossroads Primary School, Dunnet

Campsite

I was in a forest. I walked amongst the trees when I saw a tent. I crept through the door and I got such a surprise because I saw lots and lots of sweets and a chocolate fountain!
I saw marshmallows and chocolate shaped like logs. I saw colourful gummy bears in glass jars. I saw tons of brightly-coloured candy clocks that showed me it was Christmas time, and yellow foam ducks bobbing in the chocolate fountain.
I felt joyful because this was an amazing world. I ran over to all the sweets to eat some. Once I started, I couldn't stop. I ate so much, I felt sick! I ran back through the door.

Skye MacDonald (9)
Crossroads Primary School, Dunnet

Beyond The Magic Door

One day, I went to Dunnet Forest and I saw a door. I ran to the mysterious door. I tiptoed through the ginormous, titanium door and saw dinosaurs! I'd gone back in time!
I could hear flapping. I saw a pterodactyl. It was coming! I was scared. Suddenly, a T-rex came and made a breeze. I ran to the door but the door was shut. I was worried. Then I saw a key on the ground.
I picked up the key and the door opened. I went back through the door. I was at school! I told my friends and then I showed them the door but it was gone. My friends ran away, the door came back.

William MacDonald (7)
Crossroads Primary School, Dunnet

Beyond The Magic Door

One day, at my mum's house, I found a big door in her bedroom. I climbed on Mum's bed to reach the handle. I opened the door and peeked and saw a sparkling mermaid swimming in the bright blue sea!
I was amazed at the magic sea world. There were lots of wonderful mermaids singing songs. I was hiding so they couldn't see me. I was hiding under the golden sand, listening to their beautiful voices. I started to dance and a mermaid saw me, so I ran back into my mum's bedroom and slammed the door.

Ellie Fogarty-MacDonald (6)
Crossroads Primary School, Dunnet

Beyond The Magic Door

I was walking in the middle of the woods. I saw a flowery door. I opened the door very slowly and ran into the room. I saw a big giant! I was scared. Then, suddenly, I turned around and saw a whipped rainbow cream. It was yummy yummy.

Reggie Wilkinson (6)
Crossroads Primary School, Dunnet

The Impossible Magical Door

It was Monday and Kiley was going to see the river, but when she got there it was blocked by a magical door. The door was glowing brightly. So she went back home and played games and went to sleep.

The next day, she went back to where the door was and went through it. When she got to where it led, she was so dizzy she couldn't move. Then she smelled sweets and delicious candy canes. In the corner of her eye, she could see lots of red and white candy canes drifting toward her.

She felt lots of sweet candy canes and could hear lots of people laughing and munching on the candy canes. Then she went up to the people and they laughed at her because she somehow got red all over her face. She felt excited and strange because she went through the magical door!

Orla Cooke (10)

Fairway Primary Academy, Kings Norton

The Magic Door

Bob wasn't a friendly boy, he was a robber! He barged into people's cosy, warm homes, and it wasn't like he needed to, as he came from a wealthy, happy family and had a good life. He saw something unusual, a strange door he had never noticed before.

He thought, *New goodies for me!* He stepped forward, but the door moved away. He dived through the glowing, emerald-green opening. He didn't know what he was looking at. There was a strange figure. It was dark and scary and he could see his breath in the wind.

The figure said glumly, "Come, I shall help you change."

Bob smirked. "Why should I? I've done nothing wrong."

The person said, "I'm going to show the consequences of your mistakes. I'm your guardian angel, I'm Angelina, you have caused harm to many people."

She blinked. Bob staggered. He saw a boy whose money he had taken, crying. She blinked again and he saw a devastated mother crying because she couldn't feed her children.

Angelina said, "Can you see what you did? You have so much but still you take!"
Bob laughed. "That's a bunch of hooey!"
Angelina grew angry. "You'll never change, I'm going to send you where you can't take from anyone."
She blinked a final time. He was somewhere extraordinary. He gazed around and gasped in horror when he saw a giant creature - a dinosaur! Angelina shouted, "A year with nothing will teach you a lesson!" Bob sobbed as she left.

Liam Smith (8)
Fairway Primary Academy, Kings Norton

A Perfect World

I crept to the mirror, *again*, to ensure I wasn't crazy. Nope! Before my eyes was a door, one that wasn't in my room, only in the mirror. I felt like screaming, running, but I couldn't, my legs were paralysed. Using all of the bravery left inside, I tentatively reached out, not expecting much.
Flash! My shaking hand went straight through the glass and pulled me with it! Suddenly, I was looking back at my room, just without me in it. Then I realised - shock drained all the colour from my face - I was in my reflection. I spun around, there was the door, right in front of me.
Hesitantly, I reached out to pull at the golden handle. The rest of the mystery door was vibrant with gold lace edges. I instantly drew my hand back. I wasn't sure. I knew I had to conquer my fear so, as my legs turned to jelly, I drew open the tantalising door!
I opened my eyes, which felt like they were glued together, to see a pristine, sapphire sky. So *perfect*! I ventured into the *perfect-looking* village on the *perfect-looking* path. "Hello!" someone said cheerfully from behind me. She sounded *perfect*.

"Hi," I replied. On I strode, passing many shops, colourful and *perfect*; a group of people, all *perfect*; trees walking the earth, all *perfect*. There were zero problems, everyone was happy, everything was *perfect*. It was horrible.
"Huh?" I awoke.
Was it all a dream, or the unwanted future?

Amber Stevens (11)
Fairway Primary Academy, Kings Norton

Kelly West And The Magic Door

Kelly West gasped as she woke up from her dream. She carefully slid her feet into her lilac slippers. They glistened in the pearlescent moonlight that was peeking through a gap in her indigo curtains. Silently, Kelly pulled her waist-length, glossy black hair into a ponytail and crept out of her bedroom onto the landing.

She remembered the man from her dream beckoning her into the old wardrobe in the attic. So Kelly dragged a mouldy, wooden ladder that had been leaning against the wall in her father's office, under the rusty hatch that was the entrance to the attic. Cautiously, she clambered up the ladder and into the dusty attic.

On her tiptoes, Kelly shuffled around, running her pale hand across the walls that were adorned with cobwebs. Finally, she felt a switch on the wall and flicked on the lights. Even though the lights were dull, she could now navigate the attic more clearly. Kelly's eyes widened as the decrepit wardrobe was lit dimly in the light. The lights flickered like fire, which only made the already creepy wardrobe a bit more terrifying. Suddenly, the door creaked open.

Kelly gawked in amazement. The door revealed a flabbergasting collection of bright stars and funnels of light. The vast change in lighting made Kelly stumble backwards a bit but, after steadying herself, she carefully stepped into the world of wonder. It was practically Wonderland. Trees of candy floss and lollipops grew. Everywhere was colourful. Kelly's perfect dream world.

Lydia Corkhill (9)
Fairway Primary Academy, Kings Norton

3026

Two boys stood at the metal fences of Area 51.
"Come on!" one boy said.
"Erm, are you sure this is safe?" the other boy asked.
"Yeah, it's fine," the first boy answered.
"Okay, whatever you say," the second boy said.
Friends Ben and Jerry smashed open the gates.
Ben was going to open the door but a scrambling sound appeared. "What's that sound?" Jerry asked.
"Just a rat," Ben answered. Ben opened the door to Area 51.
"Got the ice cream?" Jerry asked.
"Yep," Ben replied.
There was a white room the size of a lounge and kitchen. It had lots of computers in it and right at the back was a big circular door. It seemed to have an impossible lock on it.
"I bet I could open that!" Ben sneered.
"I doubt it," Jerry answered. Suddenly, Ben ran over to the impossible door and began pushing buttons and pulling levers. "Ben, stop!" Jerry demanded.
But it was too late. Ben had opened the impossible door. A bright light shone out of it and blinded Ben and Jerry. "Woah! It's magic," Jerry cried.

Out of the blue, a slimy human-like creature with a snake head lurched out from the magic door. It hissed at the terrified boys and began to creep toward them. Ben and Jerry began to run away then, *snap!* The creature took a huge bite.

Jake Bennett (10)
Fairway Primary Academy, Kings Norton

The Haunted Forest

I'm clambering up the creaky stairs in my nightie, ready for bed, when I notice something strange about the door to my room. My curiosity gets the better of me. Instead of calling for Dad, I lean forward slowly and, with caution, open the rickety door.

All of a sudden, I am whizzing through a void of swirling, ebony nothingness, streaks of light whizzing past. Then I am deposited on a grassy bank. Embarrassed, an awkward look crosses my face as I dust myself off, stagger to my feet, and look around, still clutching my favourite teddy, Timmy.

To my left, towering clusters of candyfloss trees surround me and jagged mountain peaks penetrate the sky, coated in crimson specks of snow. A babbling stream of chocolate swirls and flows down the side of the mountains. Jubilant creatures scurry from side to side, happily chirping and squeaking to each other.

I turn to my right, in stark contrast, I see skeletal pines cloaked in shadow, needles carpeting the ground in decay, where I hear eerie sounds - piercing screeches, dreadful moans, and a scratchy noise that gives me goosebumps. Bats are dodging in and out of the gloomy clouds.

I shudder and pull my nightie closer. My stomach lurches at the thought of what might be hiding in there, ready to drag me down to hell. An invisible force takes control over my stream of thoughts. I walk aimlessly to the right and enter the haunted forest...

Georgia Earp (10)
Fairway Primary Academy, Kings Norton

Land Of Legends

As the darkness swallowed the light, Stacey and Tina went to the shops. As they walked slowly back home to their mighty mansion, they both saw a majestic ancient door that was locked with chains surrounding it. They both tiptoed to the majestic door and climbed over the cold chains. They looked around and found a mysterious key lying on the rough, bumpy ground.

Tina picked up the rusty key and inserted it into the door and twisted it open. They both gazed over to see if anyone was spying, but no one could be seen for miles. They gazed back at the door and pushed it open. As they took their first step, there was a big cloud before them that blocked their vision. They finally were brave and took more steps and their jaws dropped.

They walked past a shower of glistening crystals and a group of flying lions that guarded the land. They had confused looks on their faces. In this mysterious land, they saw flying and talking unique creatures. One odd-looking elephant asked why they were there and the girls replied, "We are here to explore."

The elephant took them around the Land of Legends before whispering, "Quickly, leave before midnight. As the sun rises, we all turn into stone." Shocked by this, they quickly explored the vicinity and ran as fast as a flash, back home before light had struck. The two friends promised never to reveal their secret again.

Aleeza Imani Uddin (10)
Fairway Primary Academy, Kings Norton

Santa's Workshop

It was a cold winter afternoon. I was sitting at my desk, reading my favourite book, when I noticed a shiny, twinkling light coming from under my bed. I crawled under to take a look and that's when I saw it - a door with shining bright stars that said, *Magic Door.*

I was scared and excited, but I opened the door and stepped through. I could hardly believe my eyes. I was at the North Pole, standing in the middle of Santa's workshop! "Wow!" I whispered quietly. I could see toys and elves and machines everywhere. Christmas music was playing loudly, there was lots of singing and laughing going on. It was exciting, magic, and just amazing.

I started walking around the workshop. A little elf came and took my hand and said, "Follow me." He led me outside, it was so cold. There was a group of elves having a snowball fight. I joined in, it was so much fun! They asked if I wanted to build a snowman. We then spent hours building the biggest snowman I'd ever seen.

I was very cold, so the elves took me to a little gingerbread house where we warmed up by the fire, had hot chocolate and marshmallows, and baked cookies with Mrs Claus.

I soon felt very sleepy, so the elves gave me some pillows and a big warm blanket and I drifted off to sleep with the biggest smile on my face. I'd had the most amazing, magical day ever!

Tilly Checkley (8)
Fairway Primary Academy, Kings Norton

The Magic Door

Once, in an old, shabby, broken-down house, there was a mysterious door and nobody knew where the door led to. But, one night, I managed to pluck up enough courage and bravery to enter the door. Once inside the door, I saw an incredible sight of a gloomy, navy blue merged into a dark, misty purple.
As I came closer to the end of the passage, there was a brilliant flash of white and I closed my eyes in amazement. Afterwards, I looked at my hands, then I realised they looked like a Japanese drawing! It was at that moment that realised I had entered Anime Land!
I looked at my thigh and instead of having my iconic belt, in place of it was a glimmering sword resting neatly in its sheath. And instead of my favourite Sonic jumper was a yukata. I felt my, what was neatly side-parted, hair which was now an abomination of spiky hair. And from my knowledge of anime books, I thought I saw Conan Edogawa from Case Closed and Tanjiro Kamado, Sabito, Urokodoskia, Makomo and Nezuko from Demon Slayer.

I could hear the shouting of Japanese words and I could hear the smooth breeze whistling through my ears. I heard the sound of the steaming waterfall fading off into the distance. As I started making my way towards the bustling town, the wind started whipping my face. I'd made an incredible adventure.

Joshua Castle (9)
Fairway Primary Academy, Kings Norton

Hollie's Magic Door

Let me start off here. My name is Hollie and if you are wondering, 'Why are you alone on a dim street?' Well, I am homeless and I'm a Victorian. And that very night, I spotted something strange: a new door.
I was just wandering down the street and saw an old, very ancient, black door. I'm not proud of this, but I started talking to it. "Why are you here?" I asked. "Can I go through you? That might hurt you terribly, would it not?" I giggled. Then I reached my freezing hand out and caressed the glistening metal door knob.
Instantly, I was transported through the void of time. "Woah!" I cried out. I landed in the future with a thump. As I was in the road, I had to quickly jump out of the way, as I was about to be hit. As I walked away, a young woman came up to me and asked me if I was alone. I didn't think before I spoke. "Umm, yes, I am alone," I stammered. Then she knelt down beside me. "Listen, I'm Anna. Even though we have just met, you need to know this: you need to come with me, you are in great danger here."

I looked nervously around the endlessly high skyscrapers, the roaring cars, the jostling crowd of people doing their daily work. I took a deep breath, scared, and nodded. "Yes."

Eva Hughes (10)
Fairway Primary Academy, Kings Norton

Magic Door At Leicester Square

During Victoria's reign, there was a young boy. His name was Lenore. For most of his life, he wasn't like other kids. He didn't have parents. Since his father died and his mother was taken to the poor house, things hadn't been the same. He wandered the cold streets for seven long years.

"Get back here boy!" Unfortunately for Lenore, he was caught stealing. Lenore spotted a small alleyway which he ducked into. He waited until he knew he was alone. When he turned to leave, something caught his eye. He slowly edged toward a crimson door. Hesitantly, he reached out a hand to touch the handle and as soon as his fingertips touched it, the door let out a bright light and words appeared: *Joy and happiness.*

He opened the door a slit and a beautiful smell reminded him of the biscuits that his mum used to make. He heard her singing like she used to and he felt warm inside, surrounded by a cloak of love. A small, orange spark fluttered on his nose. For a brief moment, he saw mama, but a cold gust of wind blew him away.

He wanted to know more but woke up, lying in a bed. His bed. Quickly, he jumped up and raced outside, straight into his mama. He knew what the door could do, it had given him his greatest wish, his mama free and home.

Amber Smith (10)
Fairway Primary Academy, Kings Norton

The Enchanted Forest

There was a door in my house that had never been opened, so I thought it would be a good day to have a look. When I opened it slightly, I saw a very little sparkle. I opened it and more and more sparkles flew out. It was an amazing sight.
My first step into the door felt extremely soft. I walked some more and, in the corner of my eye, I saw a beautiful parrot flying. After a few minutes, I noticed it was an enchanted forest! I saw loads of amazing animals, like cheetahs, leopards, toucans, parrots, all kinds of creatures. It was the best experience of my life.
I walked and I met a wizard. Her name was Hannah. I learnt amazing things from her, like how to climb a tree or how to shoot a bow and arrow. My favourite was how to ride a leopard and how to look after one. Now I had a pet leopard, I named him Oscar.
Me and Hannah thought we heard something strange. It sounded like there were whining noises, so we went to explore. In the bush, there was a baby leopard that had a splinter in her paw. We tried to help before the mum came back, but we noticed that Oscar was the mum and Oscar was a girl!

We got the splinter out and we named her Flake. I told Hannah I needed to go home, but I would come back for another amazing adventure.

Arya Scurvin-Broad (9)
Fairway Primary Academy, Kings Norton

The Magic Door

You will never believe what happened the other day. It all started on a stormy, dark night. Everyone was asleep then, all of a sudden, I heard a little tap coming from the basement. It started getting louder.
I leapt out of my very cosy bed, but then I got really nervous. I crept down the cold stairs, it felt like the stairs were trying to grass on me. Crawling toward the basement door, the light flickered. I jerked to a halt. I inched forward through the gap in the door. That was when I saw it, a massive door stood in front of my very eyes.
A veil of swirling fog escaped from the mouth of the door and the gentle wind softly kissed my cheeks as I got closer and closer. Something grasped my waist tight and pulled me through. I landed with a thump! My head was spinning. *Where am I?* I thought to myself.
I looked up into the black and white sky and it said: *The Future*. There were weird-looking robots dragging me across a muggy field to an enormous castle where the King lived.

Somehow, I escaped. I saw an empty cottage. "Looks like I'm going to be spending my night here whilst I figure out a plan to escape the future," I muttered to myself.

Scarlette-Belle Tack (10)
Fairway Primary Academy, Kings Norton

Zoe And Timmy's Adventure

Once upon a time, there was a magical door. There was a girl named Zoe who opened the door. She was so surprised by what she saw. It was a half horse and half zebra, munching on some delicious, fresh, green grass. This animal was called Timmy. Timmy ran over to the apple tree and found a fresh apple that had landed on the grass. Timmy took a big bite of the apple and turned into a rainbow half horse half zebra. Zoe ran over to Timmy and asked, "Can I jump on your back?"
He replied, "Yes, you may." So she jumped onto his back and they travelled to a mouse's house. His house was a shoe.
They knocked on the door and Mummy Mouse opened it. Timmy and Zoe asked the mouse, "Are you having a tea party?"

Connie Cartwright (7)
Fairway Primary Academy, Kings Norton

A Wonderful Winter Wonderland

Beyond the magic door is a wonderful winter wonderland full of Christmas carolers and cabins, one for every person. The warmth swallows you when you enter, just like a warm embrace.
You see children playing so you join them. Later that night, hot chocolate is passed out to everyone in the town. It is amazing. Then there is an incredible party in the snow.
When it is over, you are so exhausted and so are all your friends, so you go to bed. Suddenly, you awaken to realise it was all a dream!

Madeline Williams (10)
Fairway Primary Academy, Kings Norton

The Magic Door

Once upon a time, there was a magic door. The boy went toward it and opened it. The boy went up the stairs and went into the monster's room, called Monsters Only.
The boy couldn't get out. The magic door was triple, super-duper locked. The boy said, "Hello, I'm Topic."
"Hello!" the monster said loudly.
All the rooms had magic doors. Topic had to say bye to Sam the monster.

Frankie Johnson (5)
Fairway Primary Academy, Kings Norton

The Scary Skeleton Party

I opened a shiny golden door with beautiful hearts on it. What I found inside was treasure with skeletons jumping around and fairies decorating the party.
The five jokers were guarding the food and every time the pirates tried to eat the food, the jokers kept on making funny faces at them.
Once I stepped inside, everyone got scared and hid behind the curtains. Some went under the table. Everyone screamed!

Safa Raza (6)
Glade Primary School, Clayhall

The Magic Curtain

One Saturday, when Gabby, Ron, and Lola were waiting for their parents, they played hide-and-seek. Gabby wandered around, it was her first time being in the house. She opened a door. Everywhere was covered in cobwebs. In the corner of the room, stood a curtain, glistening like it was brand new. She peeked behind the curtain. She heard the clanging of swords and saw what looked like a Roman amphitheatre, which she had been learning about at school. She shouted for Ron and Lola.
"Come here, quick! Look behind this curtain!"
"What? There's nothing there."
"Look again, please."
"We need to go, it's late."
How could she possibly sleep? In the middle of the night, she decided to sneak back to the magic curtain. She peeked in. She stepped through and walked down some stone steps. She heard screams of death and people cheering. She could smell the stench of blood and sweat.
Someone grabbed her and threw her into the pits. What would happen to her now? She curiously looked around and saw warriors in chains, then noticed chains on her own wrists. The gate opened as the warriors charged toward her.

She closed her eyes and, when she opened them, she was in her own bed. "Ron! Lola! Wake up! I've been in the colosseum!"
"No you haven't, you've been asleep," said Ron.
"Go back to sleep," Lola said.
Gabby looked at her wrist and saw the chains. Was it a dream?

April Evelyn Atkinson (7)
Glusburn Community Primary School, Glusburn

The Magic Door

Once upon a time, there was a small house on a quiet street. It was known as Carrot Cottage. In the cottage lived a small boy called Jimmy who lived there with his parents. He was ten years old and his parents were outside in the back garden doing some gardening, so he was all alone in the house.
That afternoon, a man came up the front path to Jimmy's house. The man knocked on Jimmy's door. He answered it. The man was a burglar and he charged at Jimmy. Jimmy ran up the stairs to his room with the man close behind him.
Jimmy opened the bedroom door and he couldn't believe his eyes because, instead of his bedroom, there before him stood a land made of candy! Candy Land was huge, it had gumdrop floors, candy cane trees and gingerbread houses. Jimmy entered and the magic door shut behind him.
Jimmy spent what felt like days, but was in fact only 2 hours, there and then decided he'd better get home as his parents would be worried. He must be safe now. Jimmy's parents called him for tea. He opened his bedroom door and there were his parents, and there was no sign of the burglar.

Charlie Cooke (8)
Glusburn Community Primary School, Glusburn

The Mysterious Door

I crept into a strange hotel as I had nowhere to stay. I approached the man at the counter. I asked him for a room and he yelled in a furious voice, "Number 42, now get out of my sight!" I rushed up the stairs so I could get away from him.
On my way, I saw a mysterious door covered in tape that said 'Do Not Enter'. There was also a note. In bold writing, it said, *Caution: Not safe!* so I decided to come back later. I went to my room and hopped into my bed, which was not comfy, then I fell asleep.
In the middle of the night, I got up and put my jacket on. I headed downstairs to the door I had seen earlier. I ripped off the tape and the note, then pulled open the door. I tripped and fell inside of it - I was flying! I landed on the ground and realised where I was. I was in a field.
I saw a button. I flew over to it and I read what it said. There were two buttons, one said 'Sunny' and the other said 'Rainy'. At that time, it was sunny so I pressed the second button and it started to rain! I pressed sunny again because I didn't want to get wet. I started to fly higher and higher until I saw something...

Summer Bull (11)
Gravel Hill Primary School, Bexleyheath

The Century Portal

Another mediocre day, dribbling the black and white ball. My garden consisted of lime-green plants and sage-pigmented trees that brought out the wildlife. Aside from the green monstrosity, there was an orange brick wall where I booted my legendary football.
Kicking the sphere at the highest velocity, I smacked it at the wall, sending the brick flying well away. Suddenly, a rumble shook the grassy pasture. In a moment, a purple portal and a blinding light emerged from the wall I'd destroyed. With caution, I proceeded with my trusty ally. To my surprise, I heard the voices of Cristiano Ronaldo, Kylian Mbappé, and Robert Lewandowski in the foreign, forest-like world. I sprinted to meet my idol. Standing before my eyes, him, Ronaldo. His glare was irresistible and his smile showed he was truly one of the best in his generation.
"Do you want to play football?" I asked. But, surprisingly, they all looked completely flummoxed! This was a strange parallel universe!

A thought flashed through my mind: *I was sent here to restore football to this unknown galaxy.* Starting with the rules, Zlatan Ibrahimovic was pumped up with a burst of excitement, and so were the others. A few dribbling, midfielding, striking, and goalkeeping lessons - they flourished. It was all a dream.

Devjit Saha (10)
Gravel Hill Primary School, Bexleyheath

The Unknown Door

My name is Archie. I'm ten years old. People usually call me Arch. I'm in Year 6.
One day, the teacher asked me to fetch something from the art cupboard. As I was walking down the corridor, I bumped into a visitor and said sorry. The visitor left, so I carried on walking until I bumped into something else.
I said to myself, "Something isn't right with me today!" I'd bumped into something hard, it was a door. A door I had never seen before. I put my hand on the grey, wooden door. I accidentally pushed and it opened. What I saw was a shocking surprise!
As I pushed it, I saw a bright light shining at me. But behind it was the best part - it was raining money and there were chocolate lakes! I could hear the chocolate bubbling. I saw someone who looked like the leader of it all. I walked up to him and said hey.
He replied hello back, and said, "Do you want to work for me? £20 an hour and a discount on chocolate." As he got me a cup to try the chocolate, the chocolate machine broke. It started to flood with chocolate. The man tried to fix it. He said to me, "One second!"

He went into the room with all the machines and the flood instantly stopped. He finally came back and said, "Do you still want to try the chocolate?"

Archie Leigh (10)
Gravel Hill Primary School, Bexleyheath

The Lost World Of Football

It was another normal day, I was playing football as usual. I tested my shots, trying to hit the paper targets that I'd hung on the brick wall. I succeeded a couple of times, but then my luck was finished. I struck the ball as hard as I could in frustration. The wall came crumbling down in smithereens and a blinding light emerged from below. I inched forward and reached out my hand to what seemed like a portal. I thought this was a dream but it was reality! I was taken to another world! It looked like a plain desert.
Out of the corner of my eye, I saw the best footballer of my generation: Cristiano Ronaldo. I asked him if he wanted to play, but he just looked confused. It was clear I had to rebuild the game of football. I gathered all the players around me and I taught them the rules of the wonderful game. All I needed now was a stadium.
I assigned everyone a task and, in no time, the stadium was finished. I became the referee and split all the players into teams. Mbappé, Messi, Ronaldo, Kevin de Bruyne, and the rest of the players. It ended in a draw! But the skills were incredible and I made history.

If only this was true. I lay in my bed, smiling after what I'd achieved in my sleep.

Gabriel Chitic (11)
Gravel Hill Primary School, Bexleyheath

Soul Stealer

I was all alone. Everything I touched felt ice-cold, but I knew I had to do it. I had to find my innocent brother. I twisted the stiff, rusty handle of the ancient wooden door and entered the other side of the main entrance.
As I walked through, I noticed my surroundings and found myself standing in a black pool of a mysterious substance. Bewildered, I turned around, only to be face to face with a giant wolf-like creature with a wide, pink scar running through its blue left eye.
Immediately, I began to run as fast as my heart beat. Then I saw a faint light in the corner of my eye. I checked if the celestial being was still after me and one glimpse told me everything I needed to know. I sprinted faster than I could comprehend. As I approached the gloomy brightness, I realised that there was an uncanny portal. A portal made of blood and bone! It seemed like a transmuted structure made up of real-life human souls, used to travel to various dimensions. I edged forward and that was when I felt a furry grey paw on my back. Darkness, the only thing I could now see. Seconds later, I fell into a pale, blank room.

Sahishnu Tamma (10)
Gravel Hill Primary School, Bexleyheath

Alcante

Our new house loomed over me as I approached. A mansion in the countryside with bricks withering away due to the biting heat. It was summer. My mum ordered me to explore our new abode, "Get to know it." I followed her command.
Inside, various antiques glimmered in the sunlight. I travelled upstairs. I was met with a stained glass window representing an otherworldly creature, pitch-black, in a sorcerer's cloak with tentacles covering his face. My eyes caught on something else, a map of the world. It wasn't Earth. The bottom corner told me the name of this world: Alcante.
I detected a squeaking sound, the source behind me. I pivoted around. The glass transformed into the same creature. This time, it had a white and gold cloak and light blue skin. He lifted his slender hands like a wizard casting a spell. He chanted foreign words, his mouth opened and inside it glowed white, his eyes too.
Horizontal tornadoes came out of his mouth. I felt my head being forced toward them. All I could see was white, as I was engulfed by the same tentacles from the first picture.

Aroosh Huq (10)
Gravel Hill Primary School, Bexleyheath

The Lost Elf

I was sprucing up my room when I spotted a hidden door stuffed behind my make-up drawer. I withdrew my make-up drawer and grabbed the door handle. I revealed the inside of the tawny-coloured door. Inside the door was a Christmassy portal! I had to find out what was happening in there.

I ran in and slid down, it all seemed bigger to me. I tried to move but I seemed to be stuck. I looked at my clothes. I was predominantly dressed in red. My legs wouldn't even bend. My head felt as light as a feather. It turned to night. I somehow ripped the tape off of me. I got an idea, I decided to take advantage of my being here.

I ran over to the living room and looked around. I saw the tree, jumped in, and started to climb. I finally got into a comfortable position and hid as far back as I could go. In the morning, the lights switched on and I heard footsteps. A girl was looking for something, she looked everywhere. She seemed to be looking for me! I had to get out of there. I tried to move but I couldn't, my arms wouldn't even lift. The girl then looked up...

Niamh White (10)
Gravel Hill Primary School, Bexleyheath

The Magical Cupboard

This morning, at my school, my teacher said to go to his cupboard and get the new books. Nobody had been in this cupboard since four years ago because something happened. So, as I took a step, I got shivers. Something horrible had happened. When I was in there, I turned to my left and saw a tiny dog-like door. I went through. I saw some shimmering lights, glazed doughnuts, chocolate, Turkish delight, and felt some soothing air. I felt like I was in Candyland. I could smell it and also feel it.

I dreamt of it that night, I was so excited. I had been in there for fifteen minutes. At playtime, we were told to go outside, but I told Mrs Jones I'd forgotten something in the cupboard. She went to the toilet, so she thought I left. I told some people that I went home, but I actually went to Candyland.

First thing, I grabbed chocolate from this kind girl. Her name was Liliath, she had brown pointed hair just like chocolate. Candyland had a pinky-purple galaxy surrounded by stickers and pictures. I couldn't tell my teachers, they would ban it.

Izabelle Woods (10)
Gravel Hill Primary School, Bexleyheath

The Door To The Jungle

As soon as we arrived at the new house, I slammed open the old creaky door. I was going to get the best bedroom! I stumbled across a room. Luckily, it had a door that wasn't creaky, but I fell into an unknown jungle!
Sadly, I fell face-first into the ground. But how? I swore I was in the house! It had to be a dream! As I pinched myself, I realised it was all real. I could explore. I could find something to eat, maybe a coconut. So I went to find some wildlife but then it was night and it was cold. How was it possible to be hot in the day but cold in the night?
Now I was lonely in the deserted jungle. Hopefully, I wouldn't trip on the tangled vines, or on the roots that stuck out of the ground. I woke up covered in dirt. I watched the amazing wildlife, like tropical birds such as amazing parrots. But they kept flying too low.
I had to get back, so I ran. Once I got there, the door was on top of a stupid tree. So, not only I fell from the tallest tree, I had to climb it. I managed to climb up. I opened the door to see the hallway.

Poppy Delatauche (10)
Gravel Hill Primary School, Bexleyheath

Once In A Century

Hesitantly, I stood in front of the door while questioning whether I should turn the knob and reveal the secrets behind it. Curiosity took over me. As I turned the knob on the bulky door, I was shown a new realm of an unknown species. Was this possible?
Pairs of eyes looked at me as if I was the animal. Fear and excitement loomed over me, I was unsure what to do. The only words that appeared in my mind were: stay still and don't move a muscle. I blinked and, out of nowhere, there stood a lion. It was rather big and looked like it would pounce on me and I'd be dead. I feared that I was the food. The rushing sound of water filled the warm atmosphere while the mythical animal's eyes were fixed on me. The green tangled vines hung in the air like ropes, almost perfect for swinging from place to place, as the hot temperatures warmed everything up.

Ellie Le (10)
Gravel Hill Primary School, Bexleyheath

Noah And The Pirates

One day, I was opening my bedroom door when I magically found myself on a huge wooden pirate ship! It was gigantic and the floor was covered in smelly, slimy seaweed. The wind was racing and howling through the four black sails and I could see determined pirates with yellow teeth and ragged clothes pulling ropes. I could hear the steering wheel creaking and the waves crashing onto the boat. The air smelt like fresh sea salt. All the pirates seemed very busy.

Suddenly, a big, snarling pirate shouted, "Land ahoy!" Every pirate busily raced around the wet deck to pull knotted ropes, before jumping into the salty sea.

I nervously followed them. We bravely swam to a very strange little sandy island. In the centre of it, there was a ring of grass with a barrel full of treasure on top! The treasure was a wonderful mix of coins, necklaces, and crowns! The strong first mate picked the heavy treasure up and swam back to the ship. Everyone followed him.

Back on board the ship's deck, I suddenly felt a shiver run right through me because the Captain barked, "Noah, put that precious treasure in my cabin now!"

I trembled a bit, before walking to his cabin with the treasure. As I opened the door, something very strange happened - I appeared in my bedroom, where the adventure had started! I took a deep sigh of relief. No more shouting pirates... for a while!

Noah Meekley (8)
Highfield South Farnham, Farnham

A Magical Fairy Door

I spotted a strange-looking door. As it stood tall, the door sparkled and shone with the help of the sun. The door looked pale. It looked like a hand was gripping tightly.
The door opened and a princess and lots of little fairies came out. Each had a dress in a different colour. For each colour, there were so many shades. Also, there were strawberries, sweets, cupcakes, and cakes.
"Hello, little fairies," I spoke to the fairies.
"Hi, who might you be?" replied the fairy princess.
"I am just an eight-year-old girl. I found the door that leads here," I said back.
"Oh, feel free to explore," exclaimed the fairy princess.
I wandered off and started to explore. After fifty minutes, I had to leave.

Emmellie Holt (8)
Huntingtree Primary School, Halesowen

North Pole Adventure

I woke up in my cosy bed and, suddenly, I saw a tiny little door. I got up and wondered where it would take me. Would it be scary? Or would it be snowy? Would I fit through the door?
I felt nervous to open it. I didn't want to, but I did. As I opened the door, I gasped in surprise. I saw snow! I was feeling cold, so I ran to a huge building and went inside. I saw tiny elves in colourful clothes wrapping toys.
The most amazing thing was, I saw Santa in his bright red suit. Santa said, "Come for a ride on my sleigh. Rudolph will guide us." I felt amazed. I wondered where we would go...

Joseph Russell (7)
Huntingtree Primary School, Halesowen

The Magical Door

I was getting ready to go to the cinema to watch Harry Potter. As I opened the door, I didn't see the outside, all I saw was white. I didn't know what to do, so I walked out.
I could feel hard wood, nothing like the stone path. As I walked through the hard corridor, I felt like someone was watching me. A cold, wet hand grasped at my leg. I was horrified.
As I slowly opened a door, the black suspense turned to light and I was teleported. I was in a castle and I was the Queen! I had a crown and all of the people in my village loved me. But for some reason, I missed my home.

Alice McHugh (9)
Huntingtree Primary School, Halesowen

The Little Girl Finds A Magic Door

"I love going to the park," the little girl said. Suddenly, she found a secret passageway down the hill. She decided to go down the passageway by herself!
She went down and then she saw a door. She tried to open the door, but it was too rusty. She couldn't open it, so she got some big dangerous tweezers to try to open the door and it worked!
The little girl went in and read all of the books that were there. She was so excited to read all of the books in the library. "I love reading books," the little girl said.

Tasneem Mahub (8)
Huntingtree Primary School, Halesowen

Memories Of The Past

An extract

At my orphanage, I never fit in. Everyone hated me except one person who was my friend; his name was Aiden. As we sat down for breakfast, I told him, "You know, I've always wanted to leave this place and run far away."
"Where would you run off to?" he asked.
"I don't know, anywhere apart from here," I responded.
Before we knew it, it was 5pm. We were allowed to stay awake in our dormitory until the lights were out at 7pm. Normally, for that time, we would have a chat and talk about random things - like how annoying the others were but this time, I went for something daring.
"Hey, Aiden," I whispered. "How about we get out of here?"
"Are you crazy?" he hissed. "How will that be possible?"
"Trust me, I always have a plan."
Tiptoeing, we both silently sneaked out of our dorm. Everything was silent. The only sounds that could be heard were the thundering of our heartbeats. It was strange seeing the outdoors. The building was being choked by the merciless vines. Together, we ventured into the woods.

Unexpectedly, we stumbled across a door. "What can a door be doing here?" I wondered. "Let's quickly go inside."
As we opened the door, rainbows danced in our faces and we were dazzled by the shining light. Hesitantly, we stepped through. Pure white filled the empty void. I was worried about my decision. My breaths were now coming in quick gasps. "Welcome to the Memory Palace, where all of your memories are stored in this infinite room," boomed a voice.

Behzod Raupov (11)
Hurst Primary School, Bexley

Door To A New Dimension

An extract

Once upon a time, there were three boys playing Super Tails Odyssey. "Press C, Press Y, Press C!" exclaimed Tim.
"Okay, okay, okay," moaned Bob.
"OMG, you did it!" shouted John, who was sitting there watching them. They were jumping up and down with happiness. Then it was school time.
"Hey, babe," someone said.
"Who the heck is that?" asked Bob and John, feeling really confused.
"Oh, that's my girlfriend, Joanna," replied Tim. Then Tim noticed something, it was a random door in the middle of the pavement. "I wonder what happens if you go into that door?" questioned Tim. Tim and his friends went over to the door. All of them were scared to open the door, but they opened it and Bob threw his copy of Super Tails Odyssey in there. What they heard was shocking.
"Ow! What is Super Tails Odyssey? What a rip-off of Super Mario Odyssey!" shouted a random person.
Then Bob pushed all of them into the door and jumped in.

"Who are you?" he shouted again.
"My name is Tim. That is my girlfriend, Joanna. These two are my friends, Bob and John," Tim explained, feeling a bit frightened.
"My name is also Tim," said Tim 2, feeling a bit suspicious. "I recommend taking off your shoes," recommended Tim 2.
"Why?" asked Tim 1, feeling confused.
"Because of this..." answered Tim 2. Tim 2's mum kicked down the door.
"*Ahh!*" all of them screamed. They ran toward the door, but it'd disappeared.

Callan Humm (10)
Hurst Primary School, Bexley

The Adventures Of Mack

An extract

One day, Mack was taking a walk when he saw a mysterious white door with green stars on it. He opened it and stepped inside. The room lit up in white, then he heard a voice saying, "Wake up!"
He woke up and screamed in terror, "Where am I?"
Then the tourist shark answered, "You're in Sharktropolis."
Surprised, he stood up and ran away, saying, "Catch me if you can!" And he ran away.
"Come back!" shouted the tourist shark, chasing after Mack. Shockingly, the tourist shark caught him.
He replied, "Oh no, you caught me." He'd got to the east end of Sharktropolis.
The shark tourist asked, "Do you want a tour?"
Surprisingly, he answered, "Yes, please, I would like to take a tour."
"All aboard the tour bus!" he replied. "First stop: Shark Woods Academy."
The bus started to move and they saw Shark Woods Academy. "Wow, it looks amazing," said Mack. The next stop was going to be announced, so Mack wanted to know more. The next stop was the Statue of Shark Liberty.

The tour bus stopped and announced, "All tour people, please feel free to collect souvenirs before we continue our tour." They had souvenirs like hats, shirts, and wallets. The last stop was Shark Plaza, the tour people's favourite destination.
The shark tourist's name was Damian. After the tour, Mack asked Damian, "Can I stay with you?" He answered with delight, "You can stay in my two-bedroom apartment!"

Jasper Jones (10)
Hurst Primary School, Bexley

A Different World

An extract

Once upon a time, there was a boy called Atreus who lived in Midgard (Earth). He had special powers to change into different animals. He didn't know he could do this until, one day, he found a weird magical door at the end of his garden. He peeked through the door and he saw a mysterious place.
"Woah!" screamed Atreus. Smoke and dust filled the air. He fell through the door. The new world smelled like lavender and there were particles everywhere. His eyes were blurry, but he could see someone in the distance.
"Hey, you alright?" asked the stranger as he helped him up.
"Yeah, I'm alright, wait, who are you?" questioned Atreus, slightly shaken.
"Well, my name is Sindri, and your name?" asked Sindri with a worried look on his face.
"My name is Atreus and I'm fourteen. Not being rude, but why are you so short Sindri?" he asked.
"I'm a dwarf and my job is to keep these realms safe."

"Realms? I've never heard of them before," Atreus said.
"Well, they are basically different worlds, I suppose. I think you were just in Midgard. There are other realms," Sindri stated.
Atreus looked back at the magical door and tried to open it, but it was locked. How was he to return home to Midgard?
"You can't open the door from this side," said Sindri. "Certainly not without the gateway crystal." Sindri explained that you must place a crystal in the handle before you can use it.

Nathan Ramzan (10)
Hurst Primary School, Bexley

A Phone Call Away

An extract

I took one step, and I was in a room with the telly playing.
"Last night there was an attempted murder at a Chinese restaurant named The Silk Dragon. All the victims were able to escape except one, witnesses have claimed that the anonymous male is named Michael Smith. The police arrived at the scene an hour later and all that was left was a knife, splatters of blood and three bullets on the till. Here's the next-"
Ring ring! The tinny sound of a phone caught Dan's attention. "Hello, Dan Wallis speaking?"
"Hey, Dan, it's ya bro Ed. Can you come with me and my mates to The Silk Dragon tonight?"
Dan thought for a minute. "I swear something happened there last night though."
There was a chuckle at the other end of the phone. "Nah man it's fine we're all going."
Dan massaged his temples and sighed, replying, "Okay, calm, I'll see you there," then hung up.
As night fell and stars began to appear in the sky, Dan started making his way to the restaurant, keys jangling in his pocket. His friends weren't there yet, but he was starving so he decided to order some food to tide him over until they arrived.

The first thing he did was open his fortune cookie. *You are in grave danger. Escape the city quick and never return.* Dan stared at the note in confusion for a while, then chomped down the cookie and shoved the paper into his pocket, thinking nothing of it...

Flynn Ethan Wallis (11)
Hurst Primary School, Bexley

Perfect Land

An extract

She yawned, rolled over, and rubbed the sleep from her eyes. She unplugged her phone from the charger and glanced at the notifications. "I'm only 11 years old," she mumbled to herself. "My world shouldn't be this sad." Every notification linked to a story of more war, deadly disease, poverty, and stories of misery.

Her thoughts were interrupted by her mother's voice calling from downstairs, "Dog walk time, get up and get down here!" She groaned but quickly followed instructions.

"I'm coming," she called back. Truthfully, she quite enjoyed going for a dog walk.

Once out in the woods, her thoughts returned to the miserable state of the world. A loud bark from Crackers, her cocker spaniel, stopped her thoughts. She turned and followed the noise. The barking got louder and she ran toward where she thought the sound was coming from. Looking straight ahead, she didn't notice the fallen branch lying in her path. She tripped and, as she landed, sliced her knee.

As she stood up, she looked down at her cut, bloody knee, but something deeper in the woods quickly got her attention. She'd never seen it before, it was an old wooden door. The door opened with a creak and she stepped inside, unsure of what to expect. A rush of warm air immediately hit her skin, it was like stepping out of winter into the hot summer. Straight away she felt a tingling sensation in her leg and looked down. Miraculously, the cut had healed.

Phoebe Joy Silley (10)
Hurst Primary School, Bexley

Winter Wonderland

An extract

Oliver and his brother George awoke to a bang. It was 12am on Christmas Eve. They both opened their bedroom doors. *Bang!* There it was again. Peering from the stairs, they saw a big shadow. Oliver whispered, "Is that Santa or is that Dad?"

"It is Santa!" gasped George.

The boys crept downstairs. They peeked in the living room, but he was gone. George looked outside to find Santa's reindeer eating carrots. At the bottom of the garden, the boys saw a ray of light coming from their garden shed. Their curiosity got the better of them. Santa ran towards the glimmering light and, without hesitation, the boys chased after him. Through the cracks of the door was every coloured light that you could imagine. Closing their eyes, they stepped in.

As they opened them again, they discovered they were in a winter wonderland. It was magical. Snow encased the whole village, it was the most amount of snow they had ever seen. A ten-foot Christmas tree stood in the middle of the wonderland with flashing coloured lights.

Oliver and George explored the surroundings. They came across a building titled *Santa's Workshop*. They couldn't contain their excitement as they hurried toward the grand doors. It was no use, the door was locked. It was only to be opened by Santa.
While they waited, they decided to have a snowball fight. They were having so much fun they didn't realise one of the snowballs had hit someone other than them...

Oliver F (10)
Hurst Primary School, Bexley

The Magic Door

An extract

Estelle and Zora were both fourteen. Estelle had brown curly hair, hazel eyes and freckles scattered across her small nose. Zora, on the other hand, had beautiful golden locks that cascaded around her shoulders, piercing green eyes, and rosy pink cheeks. Although they were extremely different in looks, their personalities were equal. They both loved reading, writing, but most of all they loved spending time together.

One day, they were taking a stroll through Evergrove Gardens, the tall green grass gently brushing against their calves, and their laughter echoing around the wide space. They turned and, without realising, went down a different path than usual. After a couple of minutes, they came across a mysterious door. The door was surrounded by a bright shining light. They opened it.

In a split second, both girls dropped into a wooden boat upon a crystal-clear river. The river took them to the door of a grand castle-looking building that opened without assistance. Both girls stepped from the boat and glanced at one another. Both had a shocked look on their faces.

From behind them, they heard a high-pitched voice. "Welcome girls," said a tall, thin lady with a pretty face, dressed in a long, pink, floaty summer dress. On her face was a beaming smile. Behind her, stood a taller even thinner woman who was just as pretty but wore dark clothes and boots, and had hair as black as night, her eyes were mean-looking and her arms were folded across her chest.

Connie Batten (10)
Hurst Primary School, Bexley

The Magic Door

An extract

One cold day, I was walking home from school but then heard something, a unique noise, something peculiar. I followed the strange noise and found a door that shone a very pale blue. I opened the door carefully, trying not to be seen, and saw a mystical winter wonderland. I was overwhelmed by the sight and swiftly went home to grab my gloves, hat, coat, and earmuffs, preparing to wander this strange land.
I ran back into the woods to find the peculiar door and went through. I saw a palace made of ice, though never melting; princesses ruling the lands around them; and much more! I could feel the icy winds blowing on my face. I quickly ran to one of the princesses and asked, "Where am I?"
"A winter wonderland!" replied the princess, who seemed to be forcing her happiness.
I decided to explore and look around, there seemed to be everything anyone could dream of! The princess approached me, frightened, and said, "You can't be here for long, there's no escape if you stay too long."

Shocked and confused, I replied, "Why would I want to leave? This place is amazing!"
But the princess seemed surprised by my answer, the shock on her face began to scare me. "You don't know the story do you?" She paused.
"Of this place and its origins?" she said slowly.
I suddenly remembered, "No, no, no. I have to leave. If I'm here too long I'll freeze."

Scarlett Moore (10)
Hurst Primary School, Bexley

The Magic Door

Suddenly we crash-landed on Earth. "Where are we?" said the captain as we walked on Earth. Then *boom.* It was none other than the villain Black Hood.

"Well, well, well, if it isn't the one and only Captain Keiran."

"You!" he said. "I will destroy you."

"Oh really?" said Black Hood.

The disaster struck. One of the crew members was hit by a stink bomb.

"No! Why did you do that?" said the Captain.

"You deserve payback. Remember two years ago you made fun of me. You laughed while I tripped over," said Black Hood. "So now I will kill you without any help." Then Black Hood stabbed the Captain.

"No!" said the Captain. "You will never kill me."

"Oh? Who is going to help you?" said Black Hood.

Then out of nowhere came Super Captain. "Hey Black Hood, take this!"

"Ow!" said Black Hood. "This is the last I will see of you."

Black Hood got hit. Now time for the final battle, Captain Kieran vs Black Hood. The battle began. "Ha! You are weak, I am strong," shouted Black Hood. Then out of the dust came the crew member!

"You're alive!" said Captain.

"I am." Then Black Hood got hit in the face by the crew member. "It is over now," said the Captain. *Boom.* Black Hood was destroyed... or was he?

Keiran Connelly (10)
Hurst Primary School, Bexley

The Evergreen Door

An extract

I didn't know what happened. One minute, I was walking through the Evergreen Forest and the next minute, I fainted and awoke before a pair of ancient oak double doors. Firstly, I was walking in the forest with my friend, Jack, and, all of a sudden, we heard a crunch underfoot. I thought it was just Jack walking into a pile of leaves but then I realised, there were no leaves.

Cautiously, I swivelled around, only to see a black silhouette staring dead at us, only a few metres away! Without thinking, we ran. "Where are we going?" I heard Jack shout.

I screamed back, "Just run!"

Jack didn't understand why but when the black hand curled around his shoulder, it didn't take long for him to realise that running was the only possible solution.

The next morning, I found myself lying beneath a tree stump. I was really, really hungry. Then I heard quiet nibbling as if somebody was eating... I didn't think, the cake was already pried out of Jack's hand and stuffed into my parched mouth. Then, suddenly, I fell! Everything went black. I finally awoke in front of a large pair of ancient double doors.

I took a while to examine them, their ornate and beautiful carvings of Roman gods and goddesses, their stunning golden hinges, and everything in between. I slowly and cautiously opened the heavy oak doors and inside I saw a desert! There was nobody there. It was a desolate, barren wasteland.

Evie De La Porte (11)
Hurst Primary School, Bexley

World Of Nothingness

Ash looked at the clock as the last few minutes of the school day drained away. Finally free from the classroom, Ash began the familiar walk home. Suddenly, she realised it was quiet and she hadn't seen or passed anyone for quite some time. "It's fine," she told herself. "Nothing to worry about." Even so, her pace quickened, she was eager to get home.

However, the sight of home made Ash stop in her tracks. Her lovely, safe, and welcoming front door was glowing bright yellow! Thoughts buzzed through Ash's mind. What was causing this bright glaring light? Ash suddenly felt herself being pulled toward the door. She held her breath, her hands trembling. What was happening?

Ash closed her eyes, waiting for the pulling sensation to be over. Suddenly, even through her closed eyes, Ash could see the blinding light had dimmed and she could open her eyes. She was on the other side of her front door, but she was horror-struck to find herself far from home.

She gazed all around her, but a thick mist hung in the air. She walked forward, arms reaching out for something, anything. Ash was petrified to realise she was within an empty nothingness.

She was becoming more desperate to understand why she was there. Then, to her disbelief, she realised she had wandered away from the door, which she could no longer see. She sank to the ground, weeping, alone, with all hope draining away.

Lilly Grace Hewitt (10)
Hurst Primary School, Bexley

Sweet Adventure

An extract

"Yay! Today is the day I get to open the magic door, I have been waiting for this for forever!" I quickly jumped out of bed and ran to the door. I stood there for a moment, taking a deep breath. I slowly opened the door, gasping. I couldn't believe what I could see.
As I stepped forward, my foot began to sink. I looked down to see I had stepped onto a marshmallow path. I took a few steps forward and all I could see was this massive slide! I was a bit nervous, as I didn't know where the slide would take me. I took a deep breath, sat down, and went for it. "*Weee!*"
All of a sudden, I came to a sharp stop. I opened my eyes and realised I had bumped into a squidgy, red gummy bear. "Oh, gosh, sorry, I bumped into you."
"That's okay, but who are you?" asked the gummy bear.
"I'm Ella, pleased to meet you."
"Hi Ella, I'm Gummy. Gummy the bear. Welcome to Candy Land! Come with me, I'll show you around. Come quickly, the train is about to leave," explained Gummy.

We quickly ran over to catch the train to start the tour of Candy Land. The train started, but I felt so hungry. "Do you have anything to eat?"
"Of course! Everything you see, you can eat. Try the train."
"The train?" I took a big bite. "OMG! This tastes delicious." I couldn't believe my eyes.

Ella Hopton (11)
Hurst Primary School, Bexley

Door To The Future

One misty November morning, Jake was walking to school when he saw a mysterious glow in the distance. As he moved closer, the glow became brighter and brighter. Jake suddenly realised that the glow was coming from a strange door. Reluctantly, he slowly twisted the handle and the door flung open unexpectedly. In an instant, he was transported far into the future.
Jake looked around confused. He saw things that hadn't even been invented before, such as cars that could float and drive underwater, robots that could do things that humans could do like cleaning, working and mowing the grass. Up in the sky, men and women, boys and girls, were flying amongst the birds; animals could even talk! Every house and building in the street was made of glass. Jake could hardly believe his eyes! Was he really in the future?
As Jake began to feel excited about what else he might see, he suddenly realised that he was going to be late for school. *How am I going to get home?* he thought worriedly. In the distance, he noticed that the magic door was vanishing before his very eyes.

Jake ran as fast as he could to reach the door, leapt forward, and managed to get through just in time before the door disappeared completely. Luckily, Jake had returned right outside of his school gate, just before the 8:45 bell rang. What a strange, exciting adventure! Jake hoped that he might visit the future again one day soon.

Bradley Kent (10)
Hurst Primary School, Bexley

The Other World

An extract

I walked down the street, my heavy boots clunking on the cobblestones. The rain, which was coming down in a light drizzle before, had started to plummet down like sharp little bullets. Fat droplets of water clung to my raincoat, which I wrapped around myself tightly.

I carried on walking, observing the gloomy, morose houses neatly lined up along the street. The front lawns were dying and the windows were all boarded up. I stopped dead in my tracks. One house stood out from the rest. It was painted in the most beautiful rose-pink, with purple flowers climbing up the walls. A garland of roses framed the door, which was slightly ajar. *Come in!* said a sign hanging there.

It wouldn't hurt to have a little peek, I thought to myself, *just out of curiosity*. I stepped onto the patio, admiring the vivid green grass beside me that was neatly lined with pansies and peonies. I stood before the entrance, wondering what would lie behind its doors.

I cautiously pushed the door open. A sudden breeze whipped my face and standing before me was a swirling vortex. I heard destiny call my name as I stepped forward.

My stomach lurched as I fell. Colours swirled around me, making my head spin. I felt like I was in between the fabrics of both time and space themselves! I was tumbling down a hole with no escape plan whatsoever; how could I have let my curiosity get the better of me?

Avaani Lola Chibber (10)
Hurst Primary School, Bexley

Room Of Memories

An extract

I opened the brown, creaking door and stepped inside. It was pitch-black, it took some time for my eyes to adjust to the darkness. The door suddenly slammed behind me. I turned around and tried to yank the door open, it wouldn't budge. Worried, scared, shaken, I began to realise what had happened to me.

I was in a mysterious room full of darkness. I had no idea what was in here along with me. But the most terrifying thing of all was that no one knew I was in here! I crouched down, feeling for the floor. My hands touched something solid, so I sat down, my trembling hands hugging my knees. Suddenly, a flicker of light appeared in the middle of the wall. I watched anxiously, wondering what it would do. I backed away, frightened, as the blinding light got bigger and bigger until it was as big as the wall. Then, as if it was a movie, the light moved and changed until it showed a man and a lady, a couple, I thought. They were looking down at someone or something. I just about heard what they said, "She's so beautiful, isn't she, Watson?" exclaimed the lady.

"Yes, Gemma, she's lovely," replied Watson. "But what shall we name her?"
"How about Emily?" Gemma questioned.
"That's a wonderful name," Watson said happily. "Our little Emily."
The light faded and I realised, these were Emily's memories!

Phoebe Wisniewska (10)
Hurst Primary School, Bexley

The Secret Jungle

An extract

Last week, we went to stay with our nan. I suppose you think that's normal, that's where you're wrong. Our grandparents are different, they don't take us to the shops. Instead, they lock us in a room and we have to escape in under five days otherwise... I'm not sure. I wonder what it'll be this week. Last time we had to survive in a desert where a sandstorm came every hour.
Me and my brother look at each other, knowing what is going to happen. We get out of the car and our parents speed away. Slowly, the door opens and our nan beckons us over. A shiver runs through my spine and I think my brother feels it too. Our nan opens the corridor, or Corridor of Doom as we call it. She moves behind us and pushes us in.
We fall probably 100 metres down. I hit my head on something. When I wake up, I'm in a jungle but it doesn't seem like a normal jungle. I could swear I see a gigantic bee. Wait, where is my brother?
"Calum!" I scream. "Calum, where are you?"
"Cenna!" he screams back. It sounds like he is in a tree.

"Get down now!" I shout. "We need to get out of here."
"But how?" he questions.
"I haven't figured that out yet, but I will. I just need to find out where the door is."
"Okay, we won't find it sitting around," he says, so we start looking.

Ava Carr (11)
Hurst Primary School, Bexley

The Magic Door

An extract

"Brooklyn, your detention is one hour, starting now!"
Great, she thought. She started picking up books and flicking through them, putting them back.
There must be a way out, Brooklyn wondered. That was when she saw a very dirty book. All the boarding school was dirty and scratched, but the library books were always being used because the beds were uncomfortable and you barely got any sleep, so none of the books were dusty.
She pulled it off the shelf. It wouldn't come out. She tugged until she felt a button. She pushed, curious what would happen. *Swoosh!* It was a magic doorway to a secret passage! All she could see were fiery scarlet steps leading down. She was petrified but she couldn't go back now, so she tiptoed down the stairs, scared for her life, wondering whether this would be the end of her.
It was just a room. There was a book lying on a stool. She walked over, peeking into the book. It said: *Wish for what you truly desire, take a step into the magical door, but remember these words to get back when your life is changed: trace pace laces up.*

She knew straight away what she wanted: she wished for her dad to be back and truly love her family.
In the blink of an eye, she was there in flesh and blood. She was a little girl, two years old again, but she knew what would happen soon. How could she change it?

Poppy Corley (10)
Hurst Primary School, Bexley

The Magic Door

An extract

The door emerged from the wall, gradually rising to the surface. It was a rich beige with a shiny brass knob. It swung open and I was met by a bright, blinding light. I shielded my eyes until it subsided. As I removed my arm from my eyes, I noticed the door opened into a blank, open space that seemed to continue on forever.
Suddenly, I was sucked in. I slid across the floor toward it, screaming. I grabbed onto one of the drawers and tried to pull myself up but my hand slipped and I fell into nothingness.
A vast expanse of blue stretched out before me, tranquil, not a ripple floating through it. Seaweed sprawled across the edges of cliffs, reaching out. A burst of colour cut through the water, swiftly twisting and turning. Fish, their scales shone. Unexpectedly, a sweet song erupted from thin air. A melody that melted my heart. Great masses of green land appeared, gliding through the water were turtles, their round shells sparkling.
The turtles and fish galloped downward, fleeing, vanishing behind great lengths of seaweed. I went down after them, reaching the fields of seaweed.

I took a deep breath, then went in. The seaweed grasped and clung onto my clothes as if warning me to stay and not go any further. The thought was wedged in my mind. I pondered, then pushed on. The singing had grown louder. Mermaids came to greet me, locks of their hair curling up behind them.

Riddhisha Chakri (11)
Hurst Primary School, Bexley

A Step Into The Future

An extract

As the moon took shape in the star-filled sky, Alice and Layla strolled in the tree-filled forest. In the distance, they could just about see the silhouette of a rectangle. They ran over. What had been a silhouette in the distance now became clear to be a door. The door had a coat of paint which was now peeling off and rusted mossy hinges. It looked as though it would collapse.

Alice turned the doorknob and yanked it open. They examined what they could see through the door, but it looked nothing like a forest at all! They could see the curved arc of a rainbow. Alice and Layla stepped into the spiralling arc, it felt like they were floating. Suddenly, they were not floating, instead, they were standing on a filthy road layered thickly with leaves and rubbish.

They were looking around to see where they were, and they found a house. But, strangely, the house was abandoned. As were all the other houses. They then realised they were at their house, 324 Beckley Rd, England. But why was no one in any of the houses? Why were all of the doors left open?

That's when they stopped thinking and froze as though they had been turned to stone. They could hear footsteps coming down the stairs. They ran and peered through the window, wondering who or what it was. Soon, a dark hunched figure walked past. They quickly ducked. They heard a voice muttering something hard to decipher...

Jasmin Marshall (11)
Hurst Primary School, Bexley

Sweet Love

What is this whimsical wooden door stood before me? I wondered, pacing in front of it. It was the most majestic-looking door I had ever seen. Violet flowers and emerald-green vines grew from planks of dark timber.

"Open me! Open me!" I heard an echo coming from behind the door. With courage, I opened it slowly, awfully frightened. The door creaked and inside was the most magnificent sight!

"Welcome, Queen Candy," cried a gingerbread man standing tall like a soldier.

"I am not a queen of any sort!"

A gorgeous gummy bear grinned and giggled in my direction. Beating fast, my heart fluttered, a gush of love toward him. *Have I ever felt like this before?* I questioned, strutting over, longing to meet him. "Your smile shines like the stars!" I expressed, filled with utter joy.

The gorgeous gummy bear gently kissed my cheeks and I blushed with happiness. We took a romantic stroll through the forest of candy canes, finding the perfect place to perch. We picked caramel candy apples, sweet sorbets, luscious lollipops, and chewy chocolate cherries.

After our picnic, it felt as if we'd known each other for years! Our love grew enormously in a small period of time. He sank to one knee, taking my hand, kissing it softly. "Will you marry me?" asked Mr Gummy, patiently waiting for the answer.

Sadie McGrath (10)
Hurst Primary School, Bexley

The World Beyond Imagination

An extract

A few months ago, my uncle went missing. Some people said he went missing in his own house! Little did they know, secrets would unfold. Jack had a wife and two children. Unfortunately, they died on a boat that sank. With a broken heart, Jack would never love again.
One morning, I woke up to the sun shining in my face. I was an orphan, I had no family except for my Uncle Jack. I received a letter to come to my uncle's house. I arrived at the house, nobody was inside. I walked down to the basement and came across a glowing door. With a curious soul, I opened the door and was pulled in and transported to another dimension in another time! I was taken from my world and spat into this world. I began to search my surroundings to tell me where, or when, I'd arrived. I noticed some footprints outside a cave. "Uhh, hello?" I exclaimed.
A slow, croaky voice replied, "Ed? Is that you? Help me, it's Jack."

Gently, I stumbled nearer to the voice. Jack ran to me. "Uncle! Where are we and what is this world?" Jack looked at me and replied, "I don't know, some tribe called it the World Beyond Imagination." "Wait, what tribe?" Then, out of nowhere, men and women surrounded us. Minutes later, we were going to be sacrificed. We were going to be thrown off the top of a waterfall! Was this the end?

Daniel Ford (11)
Hurst Primary School, Bexley

I Came Across Something Special

An extract

As I was strolling in the woods, I came across something. I wasn't sure what it was, so I edged closer cautiously. I noticed that the door was slightly ajar and stars were coming out. I heard them as well. It was like an invisible force was pulling me in. I came closer and closer, feeling the scratchy grass on my legs.
Out of nowhere, I thought I heard my best friend, Zara's voice. I looked around but there seemed to be no one apart from me. I went closer to the door. There it was again! Her voice! Closer though. Like before, I turned around, but this time I saw her. She called out to me. "Frankie!" I heard her yell. I stared in astonishment at her. I was surprised to see her.
"Zara? Is that you?" I shouted.
"Of course it's me, do you want to go through together?" Zara asked.
"Okay, let's go," I yelled. We stood in front of the imposing door.

"You ready for this?" Zara asked.

"As ready as I'll ever be," I replied as we edged closer and I pushed it open.

We stepped inside, not knowing what was going to be on the other side. Maybe alien territory, maybe a different century, the possibilities were endless as they swam through our minds! We opened our eyes and saw creatures we thought were extinct! We just stood there, our eyes taking in every little detail.

Frankie Dove (10)

Hurst Primary School, Bexley

A New Adventure

An extract

It was a dark, gloomy night when Fred's house suddenly started to rumble. Thunder started to rush in, making the sky pitch-black. The door violently crashed open. Howling and banging echoed inside the room. As the howling and banging died down, it left an area of mist. In the mist, you could see a faint outline of a door with moss and vines sprouting from it.

As Fred emerged through the door, he immediately regretted his decision and wanted to turn back, but he couldn't. The door vanished. He thought, *Am I here for a purpose?* As he turned around, there was a sign that read: *For you to leave, you must recover my lost treasure!* Clearly, the door was prepared because a scythe was lying next to him. He reluctantly picked it up.

He marched through the forest, slashing and bashing vines, leaves - everything that got in his way was cut in half. He really had to be careful where he stepped because there were snakes everywhere. He saw a river, then realised there was a reflection of a temple. The temple looked thousands of years old, covered in moss and vines. Fred started to walk to it, watching out for any traps.

Suddenly, twelve men jumped out with spears and face paint and charged at Fred. He immediately turned back, scouring for cover. Now Fred really wanted to know what was in that temple. He decided to come back in a week.

Seb Blake-Bullock (10)
Hurst Primary School, Bexley

The Book That Came Alive

An extract

Penelope gasped as she saw a door hiding under the wallpaper. "What's this?" she questioned.
"Only someone special can open it, have a go!" Gran exclaimed.
As Penelope twisted the handle, she looked back at her grandma, giving her a reassuring look. The door opened. Penelope wondered, if she went in, would she come out the same person? The last few words she heard her grandma say were, "Go for it!" so she did. Little did she know what awaited her.
She saw no way back home, all she could see was a beautiful woodland. She was in shock when she saw all the characters from her most recent book there. That was when she realised, she was in her book! She knew where to go, as this was the exact place and time the main character, Suzie, started. So, like Suzie, she followed the path to find the magical, metal, shiny sword. She then decided to go down the opposite path to Suzie. Despite wanting to go on an adventure, she was nervous as she didn't know what would come next.

While walking down the misty path, she felt a furry creature brush past her. She looked back and saw brown fur, black eyes, and long sharp claws - it was a bear! Penelope ran through the darkest parts of the woods until she crashed into a spotty, red mushroom. She looked behind her, the furry creature was towering over her. The bear growled.

Isabella Hilton (11)
Hurst Primary School, Bexley

The Money Heist

An extract

Suddenly, a Ford Mustang came out of a car park at the speed of 120mph. The driver, who was me, had been in this world for one week. I was starting to like this world. I entered through a red shiny door. I entered to see what seemed like an office that read Calder & Co.
A blonde man who looked like he was in his mid-forties told me to go to the boss. His office was on the corner of 30 Orange St in central London. I entered to see a large oak desk. The boss was called Ian Smith, he explained to me that they were spies who covered up by saying they were accountants. They were all recruited by MI6.
"We need you for an urgent mission. There's going to be a police truck taking 100,000 gold bars to the King," whispered Ian. He switched his television on and said, "Give me the latest files on Charlie Maguire." He added, "You may not know about the criminal Charlie Maguire."
I whispered, "The one who escaped prison two days ago?"

"Exactly, he's got hold of some gadgets that are very strong," said Ian. Then a picture of a man with brown hair, glasses, and a suit appeared on the screen. "We need you to catch this criminal before he gets anywhere close to the police truck," said Ian hopefully. "We have gadgets that can come in handy. The best is the Ford Mustang GT."

Matthew Castaneda (10)
Hurst Primary School, Bexley

Ryan's Lego Adventure

An extract

Ryan was an eight-year-old boy and an only child. He loved to play and build with his Lego. Every build he made became more and more creative. First, it started as a car, then a house, then he made a city, then his own little world!
This story starts on an ordinary sunny day at Ryan's house. Ryan just finished creating a Lego dinosaur for his zoo when something went wrong. After putting the final piece on his Lego dinosaur, which was a stegosaurus, it came to life! "Wow!" Ryan whispered to himself. "That's so cool!" It was a small Lego dinosaur that had a mind of its own. Just then, his mum called him down for dinner so he destroyed it so it wouldn't cause any trouble. After dinner, he was really curious to see what else he could make. Ryan had so many ideas pop into his head. He finally decided what he wanted to build first: Ryan wanted to build a time machine! He found every piece he needed to make it. His masterpiece was finally complete.
"Oh my lord!" Ryan exclaimed in shock. It was an actual real-life time machine. It even had a computer so you could enter the date you wanted to visit.

Ryan entered the year 1007 into the time machine and the portal lit up bright yellow. He stepped into the portal, it was like stepping through a magic door. Ryan saw a Viking long ship with a stripy red flag!

Reiiz Mustafa-Akkara (10)
Hurst Primary School, Bexley

The Mysterious Ball Of Light

An extract

The typical day was normal until the middle of Algebra when an inexplicable sight struck through the transparent window. It was an unsettling ball of light, slowly coming toward the classroom. Everything went silent. Something was wrong. Then the ball of light expanded until everything was so bright, my eyes couldn't decipher what was happening.

After a while, the intense brightness lowered and I could see there was a mysterious door. I reached out my hand and... I woke up in class. In front of me, my teacher was staring, annoyed. After school, I went to the local woods when, again, I saw the ball of light. But this time it felt real. Again, the mysterious door appeared after the blindness. Confused, I walked toward the door.

I reached out my hand, twisted the handle, and... I saw an ancient city beneath a giant volcano. Then it hit me: Pompeii. I thought to myself, *I must be in Pompeii before Mt Vesuvius exploded*. But that would mean it would erupt in my lifetime there. A few days later, I woke up. All of a sudden, I heard screaming and I thought, *This is the day I die*.

I ran out of my room, cautious of my surroundings. I tried to get to the nearby lake and, when I did, I saw the ball of light. The door appeared again. I ran swiftly to the door, twisted the handle, and I woke up on the floor of the woods, all alone.

Cameron Miller (10)
Hurst Primary School, Bexley

The Magic Door

An extract

All of sudden, I heard an almighty thud which caused my heart to drop. I was desperate to uncover the mystery surrounding the foreign and unsettling sound. I catapulted from my bed and followed the noise until I discovered a grand, magical door that stood proudly in front of my bewildered eyes.

At first, my attention was drawn to the etched scribblings on the door that appeared to be from an ancient language. As I ran my hands over the oak door, I could feel it calling my name, encouraging me to unlock it. As I fought against my inner voice, which was tempting me to abandon my better judgement, I began to distract myself by gazing at the edge of the door, which was encrusted with the finest jewels.

My first instincts were to ignore this peculiar, unwanted visitor. However, I immediately stopped in my tracks when I heard a painfully slow creaking sound emerge from behind me. My heart suddenly jumped out of my chest, my hands began to tremble and my legs nearly gave way. I gingerly pivoted to face the door and to my surprise, the door had opened but no one had opened it.

I could smell a sweet aroma lingering in the air. I could hear low-pitched sounds and I could see slight movement through the doorway. I was intrigued to know what hidden mysteries were concealed behind the door, therefore I edged closer and took one big step through.

Eliza Thompson (10)
Hurst Primary School, Bexley

The Magic Door

An extract

Amelie was lying on the mattress in her empty bedroom. She didn't have much in it as she'd just recently moved house, again! Her new bed hadn't come yet. She was on her laptop when she heard a twinkling sound from the living room. She wondered what it was. Curiously, she got up and made her way to the living room.

What was in front of her was something she'd never seen before. A magic door! In her living room! Where had it come from? Amelie had so many questions. One of them was, what was on the other side? Well, that was for her to find out herself. Amelie placed her hand on the ornate doorknob and turned it. The door opened and the other side left her speechless.

A magical garden! Amelie slowly stepped inside and immediately smelt tropical flowers of all different kinds. She could smell bluebells and daffodils and much more. Amelie could hear brightly-coloured birds singing cheerfully. In the distance, she could hear a little voice singing softly. She followed the voice and it led her to an enormous willow tree.

On one of the branches was a swing and sitting on it was a young girl. She was the person who was singing. The song was so familiar, but she couldn't pinpoint where she had heard it from. Then it clicked - it was a song her mum made up and sang to her when she was young, but how did the girl know it?

Alexandra Elias (10)
Hurst Primary School, Bexley

The Magic Door

An extract

It was an unusually cold September, so Arthur went to his wardrobe to grab his jumper. But, instead of his messy cabinet full of jumpers, socks, and underwear, there was a giant wormhole full of vibrant colours. Intrigued, Arthur stepped inside, only to find himself drifting off into a deep hypersleep.
When he woke up, Arthur heard a muffled, "Ho ho ho!" from the corner of the room. He got up to investigate and found a red and white striped door with the number 4 on it. Curious, he stepped inside. His eyes nearly popped right out of their sockets in sheer amazement.
There was a massive Christmas tree with huge decorations. There were elves, sweet and toy factories, he even caught a glimpse of Santa!
Arthur slowly made his way over to the colossal tree. He realised it was moving because it was made out of memories, Christmas memories, children's memories. He realised there was a door that had been carved into the trunk. Hoping it would lead back to his home, Arthur stepped inside.

He found himself in what looked like spring. There were lambs, flowers, blossoming cherry and apple trees, bunnies, and, most importantly, Easter eggs! Engrossed in his surroundings, he slowly walked through the meadow, secretly picking up small eggs. He was nearing Easter Island now and a tingle of excitement rushed through his veins.

Annabelle Wansbury (10)
Hurst Primary School, Bexley

The Unknown Future

An extract

Craig was relaxing in his house until two men from the military armed with pistols came banging on his door. Craig jumped out of his seat. The men demanded that he go with them without questions. Once inside an interrogation room, Commander Cliff Black sat himself down and spoke about why Craig was taken from his house. Commander Cliff explained that Craig's DNA showed he had two years to live and therefore he was summoned to fight for his country in a future war. Craig sat stunned in silence at this news. He was escorted to a room where he found many others like him that would all die within a couple of years.

Craig knew he had to escape. Craig stayed up planning his escape route. He crept out of his room, slowly but silently. Remembering the night shift, Craig dived into an unauthorised area as their footsteps got closer. A dark wooden door stood before him, giving out strange vibes of energy. He didn't know whether he should open it or run away from it, he just froze.

With the guards hot on his tail, he flung open the door and it took him to a different planet. He could see Saturn, Jupiter, Venus, and finally, Earth. He finally knew what he was going up against. He went off to explore the planet and heard cheering, clapping, and singing. He stumbled upon a large civilisation that let him stay with open arms.

Laurie Blake-Bullock (10)
Hurst Primary School, Bexley

The Life Mirror

An extract

Over 300 years ago, there was a girl called Emily. She was a normal girl with a normal life - or at least she thought. One day, after a boring day at school, she walked home when *bang!* Emily scanned her surroundings cautiously and she spotted a large oak tree that had fallen and opened a new path she'd never seen before.
Emily was a very adventurous girl. She slowly wandered onto the new forest path, thinking it was a shortcut. But little did she know where it would take her. She came across a strangely-placed door in the centre of the path. Emily was very confused, but came to the decision to open and enter.
Suddenly, there was a big flash. When the blurriness cleared, she saw everything was the same except everything was gloomy and seemed like it was cursed or possessed. Out of nowhere, a blonde version of herself appeared in front of her, looking deep into her soul. Suddenly, she spoke, "You are the key to saving our town! Please help us!" Then she disappeared into thin air.
Emily was confused. She continued to wander around. She saw depressed, sad people everywhere; burned, shrivelled buildings; and no colour or life.

Within the blink of an eye, she was back home on her doorstep. The next day, she went back to the door and it was still there. She opened the door and stepped inside...

Miley Dance (11)
Hurst Primary School, Bexley

The Haunted Wood

An extract

I wondered where on Earth I was when, all of a sudden, I heard creaking floorboards in the house ahead of me. At that moment, I realised I wasn't alone. I didn't dare move one more step. My brain was racking with thoughts. The creaks stopped. The door. My eyes were glued to it. I looked away for one second, then it was blown open. I walked forward. I was debating my options: run away and die being chased down, or explore the house, get caught, and die. I couldn't move, my legs were shaking. Bullets came firing from the floor above. I ran.

About ten seconds later, fear filled my whole body. I didn't dare look behind me. I didn't stop running until the worst possible thing caught my attention: a dead end. The footsteps were still behind me. A gun fired and hit the tree in front. I fell.

"Where am I?" I questioned, trying to move but not getting very far.

"You have seen things you shouldn't have. I warned you! Take him away!"

I was taken into a house. There was a door that looked metallic. A man raised his voice for the door to be opened. I couldn't do anything. I went in, it shut behind me.

I wondered where on Earth I was when, all of a sudden, I heard creaking floorboards in the house ahead of me... Was this the same house? Could I choose my day again?

Lily Henson (11)
Hurst Primary School, Bexley

Unidentified Forest

An extract

I would like to tell you about what happened to me during a family holiday when I was eight. So me, my mum, dad and brother Alfie, went to a holiday park called Ventor Island for our family holiday.
"Ugh! When are we getting there? I'm bored," asked Alfie as he pulled his head back from the window.
"Just an hour left," said Mum.
When me and my family finally arrived, we were so happy to see our holiday home for the week. Our villa number was 66 Sunshine Valley. Inside was like heaven. It had comfy chairs, fluffy beds, and a lovely view of the resort lake and the Sunshine Valley play area. I decided to go on a little adventure to see what could find while everyone was unpacking.
After a while, I found an old abandoned shed and decided it was a good idea to check it out. It would turn out to be the complete opposite. Inside, I found a door that was decorated with leaves, imprinted with detailed designs, and it looked as if it was carved into the wood behind it. I checked to see if anyone was looking or coming. No one was.

I turned around. Opened the door. Stepped onto the freshly cut grass and time stood still for a moment. I walked further into the room and then heard a loud pop! I turned around. "Where has the door gone?" I asked with a hint of regret in my voice.

Emily Jenkins (10)
Hurst Primary School, Bexley

The Magic Door

An extract

Past the endless row of houses into the woods. Who was she? Where had she come from? Had she run away from her home? All of a sudden, the stranger stopped in front of a peculiar door. The distinctive door was ajar, shimmering gold light was flowing out from it. What should she do? Should she go through the door or should she carry on like it was not there? In the end, her curiosity got the better of her and she went through the door.

She looked down, the shimmering gold light was just a torch. Disappointment washed over her. As she turned around to go back toward the door, it swung closed. The girl thought it was the wind but as she tried to push the door open, it wouldn't budge. Her face drained of its already pale colour. As she looked around at her surroundings, she hoped this was all a dream but some part of her knew it wasn't.

There were more endless rows of houses, but there was something different about them, ivy was taking over. Green gunk covered the floor, this was her worst nightmare. Drops of water ran down her face as she started doubting herself. Should she have run away?

But if she hadn't left home, her life would be miserable. As her family didn't love her, they probably would be happy she was gone. A lightbulb went off in her head. There was a lock for a key to go in.

Aliyah Card (10)
Hurst Primary School, Bexley

Christmas Magic

An extract

It was a cold winter night in a little village called Christmas Valley. Families were decorating their homes and the streets, ready for the big day. In one of the little houses was a girl called Olivia. Her nickname was the grinch as she never liked Christmas. Olivia would shut all the blinds to hide the bright Christmas lights out.
However, one night, she was sitting by the fire and she heard a noise and a puff of smoke came out the chimney. There, in front of her, stood an elf.
"Hello, my name's Buddy. I've come to fill you with Christmas spirit!" And with that, Buddy grabbed her hand and off they zoomed to Elf Land.
Once there, the elves asked her, "Why do you hate Christmas so much?"
With a big sigh, Olivia replied, "I've never had anyone to spend it with before, which makes me sad."
The elves looked at her with tears in their eyes. The Chief Elf said, "I'm glad I sent Buddy to get you. By the time Christmas is over, you will see it's such fun. You get to spend it with loved ones, play games, and have fun. Families are made up of all different kinds, you're one of us now. You can leave the loneliness behind."

All the elves jumped and cheered and in front of their eyes, Olivia's eyes twinkled and a huge smile appeared.

Scarlett Dunmall (10)
Hurst Primary School, Bexley

Video Game Confusion

An extract

After a long, tiring day at school, I slumped down on my bed. Thoughts swarmed my mind. Before I knew it, I was slowly drifting off to sleep. I was woken up by the dull, repetitive sound of my alarm. Sleepy-headed, I slapped my alarm and it finally stopped.

I lifted my head. I was blinded by a sharp light coming from the corner of my room. What on Earth was going on? I walked over, shaking with fear. Slowly, I was nearing the strange light. In an instant, I was swept into the blinding light and the next second, everything went dark.

I opened my eyes. As I got up, something seemed strange, different. This wasn't my house, this was a treehouse. Was I dreaming? I pinched myself. This couldn't be. I had somehow entered a video game! And not just any video game, it was my favourite video game: Adopt Me. I thought to myself, *I better make the most of it while I'm here!*

I went outside and strolled around. I could see grass and lots of houses. There were even pets going around with their owners. I walked a little more and I couldn't believe it, Francessca was here too! We went to get pizza and drove around in our cars. It was so much fun.

I was having so much fun that I lost track of time. The white, blinding light appeared again. I guessed this was where I went home.

Isla Brown (10)
Hurst Primary School, Bexley

Fairy Land Magic

One sunny day, I was watching TV and on the news, there was a new statue. I thought to myself that I should go and see it. I got my stuff and went outside. I went into the park and saw the statue. It was a dog-shaped figure. It had a sign on it and it said *Money for Magic.* I got my purse out and gave it money in the little bag on the dog's collar. Suddenly, the dog's eyes lit up and it looked down at me! The stone screeched as the dog turned around. There was a door in the dog's back! I had to look hard because it was the same colour as the dog, but I noticed a golden knob and I saw the words: *Beware! You may not touch the ground again!*

I turned the handle cautiously. I went through. I looked around. I saw bright sunshine and a mixture of mushrooms and toadstools. They were all different, beautiful colours and they all had little doors in them. I looked some more and saw tiny fairies all around me. They were flying, fluttering their wings as though they were butterflies. I looked down at myself. I had shrunk! All of a sudden, I felt dizzy. Everything went black...

I started to wake up and felt something soft under me. I heard whispering but couldn't make out what was being said. I felt frightened because I didn't know what was lurking around me.

Holly Bradford (10)
Hurst Primary School, Bexley

The Magic Door

It was a very cloudy and stormy day and there was lightning and thunder. It looked like it was raining cats and dogs because of the horrendous rain. I was terrified. I crawled into my wardrobe and sealed my eyes shut, just hoping that when I opened my eyes again, it would then just be a lovely sunny day.

Then, all of a sudden, something caught my eye. Something that seemed to be glowing! It looked like it was a door and it was cracked half-open. As I leaned my head forward toward the glowing door, I began to smell what I thought was a lovely lavender field. As I peered my head around the door, there was a beautiful lavender field and flowers blooming. What was this place and how could it possibly be at the back of my ordinary wardrobe?

Still feeling really confused, I stepped out of the door to this amazing wonderland. This was the most stunning place that my eyes had ever seen! There were tons of rabbit holes and gorgeous, adorable rabbits peeking their heads out of their holes and twitching their tiny noses. As I looked around, I thought that this was all too amazing to be true. I rubbed my eyes and when I opened them again, I was still there.

When I turned around, I noticed that the door had disappeared, just like magic! What would I do now and how could I ever return home?

Sophia Snow-Rank (10)
Hurst Primary School, Bexley

The Magic Door

An extract

I stood in front of a magic door. As I turned the door handle, I opened my eyes and I was standing on a huge brown pirate ship. I rubbed my eyes, I felt like I was in a dream.
I was surrounded by little green aliens. They handed me an old treasure map and sent me to a desert island. I followed the map through a snake-infested forest, across the hot sand, over a bridge and finally, I came to a giant tree. "X marks the spot," I said to myself.
I didn't have a shovel, so I tried with my hands. No luck there. I was about to give up when I saw a red glow in the tree. I immediately climbed the tree and found the most beautiful diamond. It was huge, red, and dazzling. I was so happy. I made my way back to the ship. As I got there, I saw a scary man with a shiny sword. He shouted, "Stop, I'm Captain Blackbeard, hand me the treasure."
Captain Blackbeard chased after me with his silver sword slicing the air. I found myself on the edge of the plank. He shouted, "Don't jump."
I saw the magic door. I closed my eyes and jumped.

I sank into the icy cold ocean and I saw the door open. I found myself back in my bedroom, the magic door had disappeared. I reached into my trouser pocket and there was the treasure. What an adventure I'd had!

Eddie Vigurs (11)
Hurst Primary School, Bexley

Gaming Wars

An extract

Not that long ago, in a galaxy quite nearby, there was a Minecraft player called Airoking who was a fierce warrior and a cold-blooded killer. He wielded an enchanted sword that could set you on fire and that could poison you.
Airoking stepped out of his ancient wooden cabin. This cabin was in a dark, gloomy forest but one bright, cold morning, Airoking stepped out of the door and was suddenly met with a crimson double door in front of him.
The door was calling him to walk through. He hesitated. Where could this lead? He very cautiously manoeuvred around the door to see the exact colossal door standing in front of him. He slowly opened the surprisingly light door and walked in. Everything went black. Was he dead? Had he been kidnapped?
Opening his eyes, Airoking warily got up. In front of him was this muscular, enormous person. He had long, platinum, silky hair. The beast had silver armour made out of razor-sharp scales. He had huge, spiky fangs and was half sabretooth tiger.

This Kraken-sized half-person half-sabretooth-tiger exclaimed that he was the so-called almighty, all-powerful Beyonder. He had brought many characters from many games to fight and see which game was the best. In the blink of an eye, Beyonder brought all the teams to where they were to fight.

Dylan Brown (11)
Hurst Primary School, Bexley

Jungle Dreams

An extract

As Timmy walked through the door, he couldn't believe what he saw. There were bright colours everywhere, it was like being in a cartoon. Giant trees in pink, yellow, blue, with multi-coloured leaves. *Where am I?* he thought. Not only was there lots to see, the noises were so loud. Noises of animals roaring and birds singing and water running. A jungle, that's what it was like. Not like what he'd seen on TV, somehow it seemed futuristic.

Timmy started to explore. As he was walking, he saw owls and birds but one thing that caught his attention was a lion roaring. It was no ordinary lion - it had three heads! Timmy froze where he stood, not wanting to be seen. He knew he would have to move to get away. As he went to run, he tripped over and let out a scream. The three heads turned to look in his direction.

Timmy's mind was telling him to get up and run. In the distance, he could see a large, tall tree. Scared for his life, he ran as fast as he could, certain that the lion was catching up to him. He scrambled up the tree. He was safe for now. He sat and caught his breath, thinking of what to do next.

Once he had the energy, he climbed up higher to see if there were any buildings or houses but all he could see was endless jungle.

Samuel Lidbury (10)
Hurst Primary School, Bexley

The Magic Door

An extract

It was a cold and gloomy evening in Moon Day Avenue, I was getting ready for bed. All I could hear was the wind howling. The trees were moving side to side and I could hear the rustle of leaves from down the street. There was no one to be seen. Everyone was wrapped up in their houses. Was a storm coming? I climbed into bed, happy to be sheltering from the monster of a storm outside, I was so tired!

I drifted off to sleep straight away. I dreamt of walking through a magical door that led to a sunny tropical beach far away from this storm. But something went wrong, and my dream took a strange turn, I wasn't where I first thought. I didn't understand, I thought I was going to a sunny tropical beach not a dark gloomy world - and there was no way out, the door had gone.

I decided to explore this dreadful world. I looked around me and all I could see for miles were rocks, cliffs, and desolation. I felt empty and alone. As I walked, I came across a cliff that towered over me and made me feel so small. How would I ever be able to get over it?

I knew in my head that there was no alternative. Intimidated by the climb ahead of me, I slowly dug my feet and hands into the crumbling, cracked rocks. I worried if I fell, no one would be there to help me.

Sienna Ross (11)
Hurst Primary School, Bexley

The Magical Door Disappeared For Good

During WWII, there was this strange, magical door that only one person had explored. They opened the door to a fun, exciting land and he never wanted to return to the normal world that was very scary and wild.
He travelled to find the weird-looking door, but it was guarded by dead bodies. He was horrified as he saw the dead bodies lying on the floor. He wondered how they had died. Suddenly, the door slightly opened and he saw an oak tree with silver leaves. Mythical creatures appeared behind the oak tree. Poppies started to sprout on the floor and then he heard the sweet sound of mythical creatures flying and dancing.
He took one step forward onto the damp grass and his face lit up with joy as the grass spread between his toes. The warm air from the blazing sun blew across his face. He was amazed at what he saw. But the door began to shrink and he found himself running toward the door. As he looked, he saw his parents waving at him. He tried to run but a hand grabbed his shirt. He heard a voice saying, "It's gone for good."

He started to tear up. He fell to the ground and his teardrops began to drop onto the dead grass. Soon, every body disappeared and red and white poppies began to grow. Soon it became a graveyard.

Eliza Greenwell (10)
Hurst Primary School, Bexley

The Lost Island

An extract

As the bright yellow sun glanced through my white blinds, the whole room lit up while the small spaces in my bedroom were still pitch-black. Nothing was heard except the seagulls' voices echoing over the clear blue ocean. I had a funny feeling in the pit of my belly that something was about to happen. My body started to shake and I could feel the beads of sweat dripping down my forehead.
As soon as I turned around, my whole room shook. Suddenly, a dark blue, magical door appeared with nothing to be seen inside. The dark blue made my room turn purple as the sun reflected off it.
Although I was still shaking in fear, I went to go and touch the cold door handle that made my hands go numb.
I slowly turned the doorknob. I couldn't let go because my anxiety kicked in, but then I could finally release my grip. I had to go through although my heart was telling me not to. Twenty random blue lines pushed me in and before I knew it, I was through.

I was shaking at how cold it was. The wind blew my hair and caused it to stick up. The place where I ended up was the island the whole wide world had been looking for. Then, suddenly, after twenty seconds, the door disappeared. It suddenly hit me that I somehow had to find my way home.

Elliot Graham Hughes (10)
Hurst Primary School, Bexley

The Door To My Future

An extract

That night, I kept thinking about what she had said. It just didn't add up to me. So, when she was asleep, I sneaked out of the guest room and went to my room.
Everything was normal, other than there was a strange bookshelf in the corner. I'd never seen it before. I let my curiosity get the better of me. I started to look through the books to see if I could find anything. I stuck my hand in to pull out a book, then something caught my eye - it was a key. It had fallen behind the bookshelf. When I leant down to get it, I saw a door. A door with a keyhole. It fit. I twisted the key and the door opened. There was a long tunnel and I didn't know if I should go in or not. I didn't want to be at Grandma's anymore, so I went in. It was long and tight. I saw a light at the end of tunnel so I kept going until I finally got to the end. I got out and I was back at Grandma's! *What?* I thought, *Have I just gone in a loop?*
I checked my phone - it was 2037! I ran to a mirror. I looked different, about 25. Was I dreaming?

I went to check Grandma's room, it was empty. "No! Grandma, where are you?" I shouted. No reply. I wanted to go back. I ran to my room, but the door was gone.

Ava Charlton (10)
Hurst Primary School, Bexley

The Woods

Amelia was a normal girl, she liked most things. One day, she was playing with her best friend, Grace. They settled in the woods as they didn't want to play in the village. Amelia was chuckling at how confused Grace was, looking for her.
She was creeping away when she fell over a willow tree branch. She fell flat on her face, getting a scratch on her face. She grabbed the tree to get up, but that was the wrong move. She opened a door! With a thud, she fell onto the other side. She jumped back with a yelp and slammed the door. She thought she was going crazy, so she opened it again. A thick cloud of mist surrounded her, and trees as tall as a mountain. But the thing that really scared Amelia was the structure in front of her. It was a circular wooden hut with a roof made from patches of fabric. She thought it was quite beautiful, so she stepped in. Her second mistake. The door slammed!
Grace raced over to see what was happening. She could hear banging. She tried telling people about the door in the woods, but no one listened. They thought Amelia had gone missing and Grace had gone crazy.

Sixty years later, she still said, "Go to the woods and listen for the bang, and you will know where to go next."

Chloe Mattin (11)
Hurst Primary School, Bexley

Magical Theme Park

An extract

I woke up like it was any normal school day. I said hello to my parents and went to get a bowl for my cereal. To the left of the cupboard, I noticed a mysterious-looking door which was brown with a rainbow outline. The door was tiny, so I pushed it open with my foot and sneaked through it.
I was amazed! It was so dark but there were so many lights flying through the air. It was a magical theme park before my eyes! All I could smell were chocolate and candyfloss swirling around me. To my right, I saw a green coaster that went straight up into the air then back down with a roar. The track lit up the whole park, so I ran as fast as I could to get on the ride.
As I was up there, I realised there was no one else in the park. It was strange but I loved it! As the ride finished, my heart was racing so I ran to the next area. On my way, I stumbled across a tree made of candyfloss. I knew I smelt candyfloss when I came through the door! It tasted like heaven. Yum! I sprinted to the attraction where you collected sweets from bushes. It was great fun.

In the centre of the park, there was a huge wheel standing miles in the air. At the top of the wheel, I could see all the neon pathways meandering through the park.

Josh Hoyle (10)
Hurst Primary School, Bexley

The Unknown

Today I was going on holiday. I was going to the Maldives. I couldn't wait! Time really did fly by. Finally, me and my family were in the Maldives! But, ever since we got there, things just felt oddly strange. My day was going normally. I went to the pool and was walking back to our villa when I saw something behind a bush. I walked on but all day my mind kept replaying the moment I saw a door. The door was oak with fungus slithering around and, worst of all, there were colossal spiders crawling around it.
The next day, I finally had the courage to investigate what was behind the door. I walked closer and closer... I was sucked in! Where was I? I walked for a while but saw absolutely nothing. My mind was blank. I saw something but it wasn't human - it was an alien! I decided I should say hello and I did. They were so kind.
I walked off and found a huge, shimmering, gold key. I picked it up and noticed something miles away. It was an oddly-familiar door, but nicer looking. I walked over there, thinking I may have found the way out.

Someone opened the door, but who was it? It was my sister! She came to save me. I had to say bye to the alien and went out.

Darcy Green (10)
Hurst Primary School, Bexley

Cake World

Once upon a time, there was a boy called Sam and his brother, George. They liked to explore the forest. They found it exciting and strange. They liked to spot the animals. One day, they came across a door that was standing up on its own. George went around to see if there was anything here, but there wasn't. George said to Sam, "There's nothing here."
Sam said back, "Strange. Who would leave a door here?" Then Sam opened the door.
George said, "What the heck?"
The door opened onto a world full of custard and cream. Just cakes, custard, and cream. Then they saw a chocolate pond. George was swimming in the chocolate pond. He noticed a sign on the door that read: *Only full people can get out.*
George shouted to Sam, "Look, Sam! Only full people can get out, we had better start eating."
Then the cake fairies appeared. When Sam and George were full, they couldn't move and the cake fairies magically moved them to the door and kicked them out.

The door then closed and disappeared. George and Sam looked at each other. George said, "That was fun." And they both went home.

George Saunderson (10)
Hurst Primary School, Bexley

The Door Of Secrets

One gloomy night, there was a kid named Connor. But he was no ordinary kid because he had superpowers. He could evolve into anything, like an exotic animal! Anyway, the sky was as dark as obsidian but then he saw a very dim light ahead. He started to sprint.
"What is that?" It was a tall figure, about eight feet and furious. He transformed into an ant and started to go over to the menacing monster. When he got close enough, he became a shark and bit his leg. Then he opened the door. There was half and half, the future and the past. He went to the past first.
"*Ahh!*" A dinosaur was chasing him! Was that a caveman carrying a boulder? He kicked the dinosaur. Then, "*Ahh!*" The Romans were throwing spears at him! He decided to go to the future before they killed him.
"*Oof!*" Connor got hit by a flying train! Now there was a yellow-spotted lizard on the train. It was really a deserter because he saw a universal portal and jumped in. Three hours later, Connor couldn't find the door. He was trapped in there for eternity.

Tommy Ruler (10)
Hurst Primary School, Bexley

A Novel Universe

I needed to find a way to escape this cavern. The only way was up, but there wasn't any ladder or rope I could use. I decided to start scrutinising the environment. In the glistening vicinity, I saw a luminous door. I caught a small glimpse of the other side.
I walked toward the door and felt a hint of unsteadiness. Then I saw something alluring. As I widened the gap, I saw a novel universe that seemed as if it was an extreme dream. I abruptly heard children yelling and screaming. As I entered the inexplicable dimension, I realised that this was Earth, but way cleaner.
One of the adults saw me and invited me to his clean and contemporary abode. As I went up the stairs, I saw a vibrant door, could this be it? I opened the door and went through. I saw nothing but desert. I saw rattlesnakes slithering around. Then everything went black.
I woke up with a scream at the top of my voice. It was a nightmare! Or was it? I looked around and saw my furniture in place. I went downstairs and saw a vivid door. It wasn't a nightmare.

Brandon So (11)
Hurst Primary School, Bexley

Lost At Gloom

Abis was different. He was into wildlife but his interest in wildlife was crazy. He had a jungle room with a leopard bed. One morning was different - his door was glowing! Intrigued, he jumped out of bed and swung open the door.
To his surprise, there was a dark, gloomy woodland. As he stepped through, he started to change. Abis' legs became four, he was hairy, and could hear better. After hearing a loud howl, he noticed he was with a pack of wolves and was a wolf too! As he was in a pack, they could hunt together which made eating and surviving a whole lot easier.
But, one day, the pack vanished and left Abis alone. But all hope was not lost as he saw a mysterious man. "Left or right?" he asked.
"Right is always right," Abis answered confidently. He was teleported back to the pack - but now they saw him as an enemy! Abis had been turned back into his human self. He ran for ages. He ran, he tripped, he fell. Suddenly, he woke up in hospital. Had it been a dream? Did this drama really happen to him?

Jacob Nicholls (10)
Hurst Primary School, Bexley

The Magic Door That Led To A Nightmare

I stepped through the door that filled my head with numerous thoughts, worries, and emotions. A jungle. A jungle with an array of trees and bushes. As I scanned the area, my eyes fixed on one particular thing: the bush. Up above, a flock of startled birds flew away in fear.
The bush rustled. The world went silent, all that could be heard was my pounding heart which echoed throughout the air. A python revealed itself, it had scaly skin that shimmered in the sunlight. The serpent flicked out its tongue to taste my fear which lingered in the air.
Moving back cautiously, I turned around just to see three other bloodthirsty snakes. They needed dinner. Trembling uncontrollably, I stood like a statue. The snakes closed in. I was face to face with a fearless python that had dagger-like teeth. The lethal snake opened its mouth which had rows of teeth that were as sharp as knives. Touch the teeth and you would experience excruciating agony. A split-second from getting eaten, I woke up panting, sweating relentlessly.

Max Slater (10)
Hurst Primary School, Bexley

The Magic Door - Battle Of Hastings

Whatever lurked in the shadows was not a problem right now. There were a bunch of doors around me, but one stood out. The handle was gold. I was very interested to find out what was behind the mysterious door, but I was worried about what was behind it.
As I moved closer, I heard battle cries. I took a deep breath, then a spear came flying through the door so I took a step back. I muttered under my breath, "Should I go in or not? Am I being foolish?" I decided to look around to see if I could find anything to protect myself.
I found a shield on the floor. I put it over my head and opened the door. I saw spears clashing and swords piercing through soldiers' hearts. As rain cascaded down, the wind blew angrily. I decided to make a run for it. I ran for shelter. All of a sudden, I was hit by a horse. As I flew to the ground, I could smell the blood as the soldier came charging toward me like a lion.
I closed my eyes. I awoke. I was no longer in 1066. It was just a bad dream.

Shea McBrien (10)
Hurst Primary School, Bexley

The Pink Door

I awoke from my dreamy sleep to find that I wasn't in my bed. *Where am I?* I thought to myself. Now that I had rubbed my eyes, I could see something in the distance... a door. Not just any old door, an interesting pink door that glistened in the sun.
As I ambled toward the door, I felt a sudden urge to just walk away. But how could I let that stop me? I finally decided to walk through the door and see what was waiting behind it. I walked through the door and it took me to a beautiful garden in the middle of nowhere. *How did I get here?* I thought to myself.
High in the sky, I could hear birds singing cheerfully. The smell of blooming flowers and the cool air weren't even the best part. The best part was the friendly animals, including elephants, giraffes, and even more surprisingly the flamingoes! I couldn't believe I had the opportunity to ride the elephants and stroke the giraffes. All of a sudden, I woke up and realised that it was all a dream.

Freya Goldsmith (10)
Hurst Primary School, Bexley

The Hidden Door

Dear Diary,
Today was crazy! I just moved into my new house but it was boring. I wanted to play in the garden because it was giant, but my parents said no. It was raining, so fair enough.
My mum and dad were working from home, so I asked, "What should I do?"
My dad responded with, "Count how many doors, windows, and stairs there are."
"Fine!" I said while sighing. So I went to count how many doors, windows, and stairs there were. Two stairs, sixteen windows, seven doors. "Well, there you are, Dad, I did what you wanted."
"Okay, now just search around for anything interesting," my dad said.
So I went off, finding stuff, all useless to anyone except my boring old dad. But, as I was looking around, I found a doll that looked like me! Behind a cabinet, I slowly moved with all my strength, there was a door hidden away. I opened it and I found a wonderland full of colours...

Finley Hopkins (11)
Hurst Primary School, Bexley

The Magic Door

Long ago, there was a magic door discovered in a deep forest called the Badwoods. Whoever went in never came back, so now the King of the land said it was forbidden to even enter the realm.
I was so curious about the door, I broke the rules and went through the magic door. The Badwoods weren't far from my home. As I reached the forest, it was dark, gloomy, and lifeless. I could hear the birds were singing loudly. Finally, the door was in my sight. For a second, I trembled in fear - but what was the worst that could happen?
I opened the door and I could feel the world shaking. I was being sucked in! I was in a whole new dimension and it was full of life. It was night and the vibrant stars shone while twinkling in the night sky. I could hear the ferocious wind howling viciously in my face. I was stepping on soft, lush, green grass. In the distance, I could see some people. Who were these mysterious human beings?

Imran Ali (11)
Hurst Primary School, Bexley

An Arctic Miracle

Gingerly, I opened the door and was astonished by the sight. In the distance, were strange figures dancing and cheering. They hopped, skipped, and jumped over to me and led the way to a beautiful, shimmering ice castle. Inside were gingerbread and hot berry juice.
Suddenly, a bell rang as it was time to leave. On the way to the skidoos, we made snow angels and saw the northern lights. The elves' angels were the best, they had experience! The skidoos were so fun and really quick. Obviously, the elves drove the vehicles. The skidoos were finished but I was told the final activity was the best...
"Ho ho ho!" bellowed Santa in a cheerful voice. I was ecstatic to see him. Luckily, I brought my Christmas list. He asked me what was on my list, so I told him what was on it. Also, he said that he was going to get what I wanted. After a long, enjoyable day, it was time to go back home through the door.

Noah Smith (11)
Hurst Primary School, Bexley

The Magic Door

My magic door takes me to a land full of sweets. In my own Candyland, the clouds are fluffy and made out of cotton candy in the blue sky. The grass is made out of strawberry strings, but instead of the colour being red it is green. The bark and branches of the trees are made out of chocolate and anything green is green-coloured strawberry strings.
Houses are made out of delicious gingerbread, then decorated with any colourful sweets such as little jelly-textured sweets, Smarties, M&M's, Nerds, and many more. They come in many different colours, with many different shades, even neon colours! The icing is white and creamy and as soon as you taste it your mouth will be filled with joy.
Now for the best part of all: the chocolate river and waterfall! You can swim in the river, eat the river, and even float in it while lying on your back being a starfish. There are no sea creatures in this river.

Inaya
Hurst Primary School, Bexley

The Magic Door

One day, I found a magic door. I went through it and found myself 1,000 years after the start of Earth. I couldn't breathe and felt very hot, so I put an oxygen tank in my heat suit and wore it.
As I went through again, I saw gigantic volcanoes towering as high as the Tokyo Skytree, rocks that were constantly jiggling, and oceans with steam hovering over them. Everything felt rough at first but when I got to the volcanoes, everything felt smooth for some reason.
When I was there, it sounded like they were going to erupt. I turned to the water to take a look and put my underwater microscope in. I saw lots of little microbes just floating around like jellyfish, eating little tiny things.
I decided to go back to the magic door to get out. But when I got back to my home, the door vanished. I thought my adventure was interesting. I didn't think I would go back though.

Iskandar Abdullaev (10)
Hurst Primary School, Bexley

Magic Forest

There was a sketchy door with steps leading to it. I was curious, so I went up to the door and I opened it. I was scared to my bones. It looked like an evil forest, there were glowing mushrooms that were the only source of light.
I saw crowds of people but they were covered in trees. I heard loud stomps coming toward me. I was going to go back to the door but it had disappeared. I was scared. Then I heard the stomps again.
I looked around me but I didn't see anything. Then I saw a big tree monster, there were loads of them. I was scared. I shouted for help but it was just nothingness. Then I was lifted up, I was being choked. I tried to release myself, then I felt this sudden surge in my body. I saw the door, then I had the power to release myself. I ran to the door and opened it. I was safe. I was relieved.

Teddy Wise (11)
Hurst Primary School, Bexley

The Candy Forest

"There's a candy tree!" exclaimed Flynn.
"No, not a candy tree, a candy forest," murmured Alfie in amazement.
As they walked through the forest, they came across a chocolate bunny gracefully hopping through the grass. As they came to a path, they heard rustling in the bushes and stepped back. A gummy bear came out and chased them!
They came to an opening in the forest and saw a lemonade river. They both jumped in and found a gumdrop. They stood on the gumdrop and jumped to the other side. They found a lemonade sea and saw chocolate dolphins and a gummy ship.
As they ran across the dry sugar, it flicked up behind them. They found a mint ship and got on it. They sailed to the horizon and found the exit from the magical world. They both left and went back to real life.

Flynn Vickers (10)
Hurst Primary School, Bexley

Ministry Of Magic

All of a sudden, Addy woke up. She heard a loud noise. She went back to sleep like the noise was nothing. In the morning, she woke up early and went to see her brother and sister. Her sister's name was Maya and her brother's name was Colin.

She could hear the birds singing and she was playing with her next-door neighbour's dog. She could hear the tree swaying. A bright, blazing, purple light appeared out of nowhere. Addy and Maya and Colin went to find out what it was. It was a door to another world!

All of a sudden, Addy, Maya, and Colin got pulled into the door. They saw trees as tall as the Eiffel Tower. The trees were towering over them. The leaves were soft. The animals felt like soft pillows. The flowers smelt like cherries and apples. The grass felt so soft.

Francesca Allard (11)
Hurst Primary School, Bexley

The Magic Door

Vanessa and Penelope were the best of friends. Every day, they would go to an old oak tree in the forest and try to spot as many animals as they could. They both loved animals and had a passion for adventure that would lead them into a world of unknown!

"I won!" Penelope teased.

"Only because you got a head start," grouched Vanessa.

Penelope looked over at a bush nearby. Something was glistening in the sunshine, but she couldn't tell what it was. "Look over there," whispered Penelope. "Something is in the bushes."

Vanessa peered down at the bush that was emitting light in all directions. The light became brighter and brighter until they couldn't see. A magical door had appeared...

Michelle Ini (11)

Hurst Primary School, Bexley

World Cup

As I stepped through the mysterious door, I felt goosebumps. The one place I'd always wanted to go, I was finally there, the World Cup! It could lead to tears of joy or tears of sadness.
I could hear the fans cheering like their lives depended on it. There was the smell of cheap beer and chips, but the fans didn't mind that because the one thing they were thinking about was winning. "Come on, England!" the fans said as their eyes were glued to the pitch.
Unfortunately for me, this always happened, an old man plonked himself next to me and began to criticise. I thought to myself, *We'll probably lose on penalties*. If you didn't know, England like doing that. What an event this was!

Owen Doshi (10)
Hurst Primary School, Bexley

The Imagination Door

There was a forest full of mythical creatures, unknown to everyone apart from one individual. That person's name was Kaci. She was an explorer, also she went on strange, scary, and fun adventures.
Kaci found a giant island that looked like a floating forest with many vines, trees, and one brown and gold door. The explorer thought there was treasure in this floating forest, but she was wrong.
There was no treasure on this island, this was called the Mythical Forest. The door was more than just a door, this was the Imagination Door! Where your imagination could run wild and free. Finally, Kaci acknowledged the Imagination Door. The key was right in front of her. All she had to do was pick it up...

Gracie Rose Putnam (10)
Hurst Primary School, Bexley

Winter Wonderland Forever

It was a sunny summer day. Lacey and some friends were playing a game. It was her turn to find them. Lacey was so hot, she hated it. She was too hot to run. She decided to take a break. When she was done, she went looking again. Lacey couldn't see them anywhere. She said to herself, "I wish it was winter."

Then, a door opened. She had never seen it before. It was snowing and there was snow everywhere. Her dream come true! A minute later, she got really cold. She wanted summer again. She tried opening the door but it wouldn't budge.

It was getting colder and colder, she wanted to go back. Lacey wished to go back. The door opened and since that day, Lacey never wished again.

Sasha Shearer (10)

Hurst Primary School, Bexley

The Wonders Of The Magical Girl

One day, a magical girl lived in her own little world. The girl's name was Polly and she had a pet called Molly. One magical day, Polly and Molly were walking in their candy kingdom when they saw a lolly on the path in front of them.
Polly was determined to taste the lolly. Polly picked it up and gave it a great big lick. Ice skates appeared on her feet! She started to skate forward, leaving her friends behind, including Molly.
There was a flash of light and then Polly appeared in a dark room in front of a glowing door. Polly was so curious that she wanted to go inside. As she got close, she fell right inside and found herself in a Christmas paradise!

Summer Gregory (10)
Hurst Primary School, Bexley

Travelling To The World Cup

One day, me and my brother were playing in the garden. It was a hot sunny day. We were practising football penalties and I was the goalkeeper. My brother had an amazing shot and I saved it! Suddenly, this door appeared next to me. I fell into it. I found out I was heading to Qatar! When I woke up I was on a pitch playing for England versus Wales. It was 1-0 to England.
I was in a high-pressure situation when Wales finally scored against me. It was the final seconds of the game and we scored! All the fans went crazy, all the players went crazy as well. I got to lift the trophy and that's how England won the World Cup!

Jack Quinnear (10)
Hurst Primary School, Bexley

The Ancient Coin

I walked through the massive door and found myself in a large park. It was a sunny day. There was a boy called Bob, he was at the park after school with his friends.
Bob said, "Look, I found a coin," with a strange look on his face. "It was on the floor."
I said to him, "Can I have it?"
"No!" yelled Bob.
We went home and looked at it for two hours. We found out it was an ancient coin from the 1830s. I would love to go back through the magic door and find another ancient coin.

Charlie Thompson (11)
Hurst Primary School, Bexley

The Magic Door

One day, far, far away, there lived a boy called George. He had blue eyes and blonde hair. He was seven years old. He lived at a boarding school. In the daytime, George was going for a walk around the school but he heard a noise coming from the basement.

He said to himself, "What is that noise?" He shivered as he ran off. George was curious so he went to the basement and heard it again. He was confused. He put his hand on the door, then he turned away.

The next day, George decided to open the basement door because he was eager to see what was in there. He saw a door covered with circles. He went in... he got transported to Bot Land which was an island far away.

The bots were really friendly. The reason he could hear noises was because they were building houses to live in. The bots were so friendly, they gave George a home. He had a great time. George and the bots lived happily ever after.

Amelia Somerton (7)

New Hall Primary School, Sutton Coldfield

Adventure Through Space

An extract

Not long ago, there was a girl named Phoebe Keondre. Phoebe was a creative girl, but she thought the world needed a bit more excitement. There was also a boy named Jake Holland, he was Phoebe's neighbour.

One day, Jake saw Phoebe planting flowers so he went to help her. They both started digging. Strangely, Phoebe hit something hard with her spade. She was surprised to see two coins that were pink and blue and flashing. When they picked them up and flipped them, they turned into superheroes!

After planting the flowers, they decided to play hide-and-seek. Phoebe went and hid behind a bush, where she found a magic door! Phoebe called Jake over and they agreed to go through it. To their surprise, they found themselves in a spaceship!

They could hear an evil alien talking about taking over Earth. She was one hundred years old but she looked very young, and cruel. She disliked humans and animals from Earth.

Once they returned, they planned to try and save Earth. They met the next day to make a plan to trap the alien. Luckily, Phoebe remembered that she had an obsession with powerful gemstones, but she wasn't sure where they could get some. Then, Jake mentioned that he had gems from the Amazon rainforest, so they started laying a path of gems to lure the alien in. Once she was caught in their trap, they threw a net over her and electrified her.

Aadya Gadepalli
New Hall Primary School, Sutton Coldfield

The Magic Door

One evening, there was a girl called Freya. She was kind, helpful, and caring. She had blonde hair, blue eyes, and was nine years old. Her favourite colour was pink.
She went to the basement to find her favourite toy. Then she saw a door. She went inside the door and she was at L.O.L. Doll Land. She loved L.O.L. Dolls! She said hello to Diva and Swag, they remembered her. She loved L.O.L. Dolls because she loved to open stuff and get them dressed.
She wanted all the L.O.L. Dolls in the world for Christmas. It was so strange to be in L.O.L. Doll Land. She had food and made friends. She loved L.O.L. Doll Land, she wanted to live in L.O.L. Doll Land. She thought it was amazing.

Lilly Eales (7)
New Hall Primary School, Sutton Coldfield

Magic Within The Forest

In my room, there's a magical door that can only be opened at night. When my sisters go to sleep, the door shines a light. When I open the door, the light is so bright, I have to put my special glasses on.
The magical forest is so amazing. I love to explore. In the forest, there are fairies, unicorns, and bears. All the magical creatures have beautiful voices. I sit down and then the show begins.
When they start singing, it's so exciting and fun. The fairies sprinkle glitter on me! While the fairies are sprinkling glitter on me, the unicorns are dancing with joy. The bears knit me a cosy blanket. It's time to go!

Liliana Cook (8)
New Hall Primary School, Sutton Coldfield

Somewhere Magical

Once upon a time, there was a girl named Lucy and she loved exploring. One day, she woke up early and it was pitch-black outside. She took a torch and went outside.
She walked a long way and got really tired. She walked and walked until she found something - it was a door! Not any door, a magical door! First it went up, down, left, and right, then it stopped. Lucy quickly walked into it in case it did anything else. She opened the door and she felt like she was in a whole different world. The sky was light blue, there were colourful hills and tall flowers.

Anjola Ajayi (8)
New Hall Primary School, Sutton Coldfield

The Zoo On The Moon

Once upon a time, there was a magic door but no one knew what was in it. Isabelle and Grace went into the magic door and saw a moon with a zoo. Grace went to the zoo to see the animals.
There were moon snakes and meteor parrots and they wore astronaut helmets because it was the moon. Isabelle went walking around the moon - or should I say floating around the moon?
Isabelle and Grace had so much fun, they never ever went back home! In the end, Isabelle and Grace made a floating house and cared for the animals. They lived happily ever after.

Halle Hart (8)
New Hall Primary School, Sutton Coldfield

The Magic Door

Long, long ago, there was a magic door that could take you anywhere in the world. There was a boy named Shovoy, he was an explorer. He had a magic door. He turned it to the past and jumped in.
Shovoy felt a scaly beast. What was it? Shovoy saw a dinosaur! Shovoy met a T-rex and he heard a fearsome roar! Somehow, the T-rex spoke, "I want to have friends, I'm so lonely."
"I will be your friend," said Shovoy.
"I want more friends!"
"Okay, I will help you," said Shovoy.

Zynlond Hewitt (7)
New Hall Primary School, Sutton Coldfield

The Magic Door

Once upon a time, there was a girl who didn't believe in magic. One day, while she was in her room, her door looked shiny and sparkling. She opened the door and stepped inside, she found herself in a winter wonderland.
She saw lots of people having fun. Some were riding the giant wheel swing. Others were skating on ice. A few were playing with shooting games. She enjoyed her time and went through the same door back to her room. Now she believes in magic and was telling the story to all her friends.

Yassin Elmor (7)
New Hall Primary School, Sutton Coldfield

Winter Wonderland

Once upon a time, a little girl had just woken up.
Her name was Lily. She was very kind and helpful.
Once she'd woken up, she found a door.
Lily was scared. She was terrified, but she had to
open the door. She opened it and it looked fun.
She went in. She did it, she was so excited, she
knew she could do it.
It was beautiful. She really wanted presents this
year. Lily was very excited. Lily went back to bed at
night time and had a dream about the presents
behind the door.

Georgia Bartram (7)
New Hall Primary School, Sutton Coldfield

The Magic Door

The magic door is taking me to swimming today. There will be lots of water and people enjoying the pool. I will have lots of fun.

Lily-May Spencer (7)
New Hall Primary School, Sutton Coldfield

Into The Future

Me and my friend, Ava, opened my bedroom door and... it was magical! The door was sparkling with glitter and it was pink inside. The door was sucking us in. We tried to go back to bed but we got sucked in!
We were outside, there was a new playground. It was not small! It was bigger, like an adventure park, a park with lots of stuff. We heard birds in the trees, it was like a welcoming song. Then I felt Ava shivering from the cold so I said, "Why don't we go inside?"
We went into my house. We smelt the smell of pancakes. Then a person flew to us with wings and said, "Hello, welcome to the future!"
Me and Ava said, "The future! That's why the playground was so big."
But the person said, "Ssh! They can't hear you or see you."
We said, "Oh!" then we went quiet. We asked, "Can we whisper?"
He said, "Yes," in a grumpy voice. He said, "Have this magical ball, when you click this button, you turn invisible."

So we clicked the button and turned invisible. We went to the kitchen to get pancakes. Grabbing the pancakes, we pressed the button by accident and we got caught!
Then ourselves said, "Look! It's us when we were nine."
We said, "Uhh, hi!" Then we ran to the person and said, "They saw us!"
He said, "Calm down, go through this door and you will be home. They will forget."

Lena Larysz (9)
Portlethen Primary School, Portlethen

Tech Football World

In the evening, I went to my football club. When I opened the door of the car, I got blinded! After the light disappeared, I was thinking, *What is happening?* Slowly, I started peeking, then I suddenly fell!
I woke up from the fall. It wasn't easy to get up because I felt frightened. I'd somehow ended up in a... tech football world. There were lots of football players, it was like a video game.
Suddenly, the football players went to fight with some super gadgets that transformed them into fit, cool, strong and smart. They also had a cool tech football! The tech football could defeat anything. But who were they fighting with? Some weird, red, spiky ball that never gave up! The red, spiky, weird ball was a virus!
I came to see and save my idols. Still, it was very hard. I definitely needed some armour. I asked one of the footballers, I whispered, "Where did you get the gadgets from?"
He whispered, "I have some." He gave me them. Then I started to transform! I started to levitate! The virus came in but I was ready. I got into a fight with the virus. I finally defeated it! Every football player was celebrating. Then I was reminded that I needed to go home.

I ran as fast as I could. I went through the magic door. I was teleported back to the car. I thought nothing happened and I was daydreaming, but no - I took the gadgets!

Fabian Mlodzikowski (8)
Portlethen Primary School, Portlethen

The Magic Door

I walked through the magic door and I was in medieval England and I was in knight's armour with a golden shoulder pad. But this was wrong! It looked like something evil was there because the sky was super shadowy. Suddenly, I heard a voice behind me, it said "If you want to get back home, you must defeat an evil wizard!"
I turned round and saw a goblin. It was green, up to my waist, and held two razor-sharp daggers. I heard him say, "But first you need a weapon, you can't fight the wizard with nothing, can you?" The goblin led me to a stone with a sword in it. The goblin said, "Take the sword out of the rock." So I did.
I pulled it out like a knife in butter. I wondered why no one had taken this before. The goblin said, "You are now the King of England because that was the legendary sword Excalibur." It was glistening with multi-coloured jewels. "Let's go to the wizard's lair."
Three hours later, we approached the wizard's lair. It was dark and spooky. But then a Cerberus attacked! The goblin said, "You go, I've got this!" So I slid under the Cerberus and into the wizard's lair.

The wizard said, "Goodbye, King!" so I threw Excalibur at the wizard and, in a blink of an eye, I was back, just in time for tea.

Harry Bruce (9)
Portlethen Primary School, Portlethen

Candy Land

I walked through the magic door and I saw giant candy canes. I felt marshmallows below my feet and I smelt melted chocolate. It was a chocolate fountain! Behind it was a candy house. I had to be in Candy Land!
I explored around. It looked like there was a tasty chocolate river that led from the chocolate fountain. There was a marshmallow boat. The marshmallow boat looked like it came from my sweetie collection!
I went on the marshmallow boat. It led me to a candy castle, it looked like a rainbow. But there was a small orange who was trying to turn Candy Land into Fruit and Vegetable World. The small orange had a giant machine that was going to destroy Candy Land!
The only way to defeat the overpowering machine was to... switch it off! As simple as that! But once again, there was a problem: whenever you tried to switch it off, you needed the little orange's face scan. So I thought, *Why don't I trap him?*

I set a trap with a sign that said, 'Put your face in front of this screen and you will get free Wi-Fi!' and it worked! The machine was off! No more fruit and vegetables!

Clark Gellatly (8)
Portlethen Primary School, Portlethen

The Magic Door

Yesterday, I found a strange door up in my attic so thought to myself, *Should I open it or not?* I decided I should open the door. As I slowly opened the door, it loudly creaked. It smelled like a jungle or something. I went in.

The door slammed! I tried opening it but it didn't work. I was scared. I heard a wolf howl. I knew I had to stay the night, so I had a look in my pockets. I found a lighter. I was so happy, I could light a fire to keep myself warm and maybe make food. In the distance, I saw a jungle. I started to head to it.

I barely made it, my feet were about to fall off, so I took a rest. I sat down on a tree stump. I felt something crawling down my arm. It was a centipede! I was jumping up and down until it flew off, but suddenly I heard rustling. I got the lighter out of my pocket.

I lit a stick and I held the stick in my sweaty hand - but it was a jungle frog. I knew it was poisonous, so I slowly walked away. I saw some kind of house. I was so excited but I knew it might be dangerous, so I ran there and opened the door. As it slowly opened... it was my room!

Dylan Zakonov (9)

Portlethen Primary School, Portlethen

Jurassic Land

As I opened the magic door in my school, it took me back in time to a land with dinosaurs! As I walked in, I couldn't believe my eyes. There were so many dinosaurs!

As I walked around, I heard a huge roar. I didn't know what dinosaur it was coming from until I saw... it was a T-rex! It had huge eyes, sharp teeth, with blue and green skin. I ran as fast as I could until I came to a dead end. I screamed as loud as I could until the T-rex stopped.

"Why did you stop?" I asked.

"Why wouldn't I? I'm the friendly dinosaur," the T-rex said as he picked me up.

"Can you show me around?" I said.

As the T-rex was showing me around, I decided to feel around the T-rex's scaly back. As I was feeling the T-rex's back, I saw the magic door in the sky. I told the T-rex and he decided to help me up to the magic door.

As I walked back through, it was the end of school so I ran to my class. I got my schoolbag and left the school. "I hope I go back there," I said. But at least I had a new friend.

Kian Jack Craik (9)

Portlethen Primary School, Portlethen

The Magic Door

Last week, I found a magic door in my room. My curtains were blowing so hard, I could barely see. Then I fell in. Why was it so cold? It looked like the north pole.
I didn't know what to do. I was all alone. I saw something... oh my! It was Santa! I wished I had my camera. I needed to focus. I needed to meet Santa or I'd be stuck there forever. I was freezing.
"Over here!" He didn't hear me. I thought he was going home... wait a minute! *The North Pole: This Way!* I smelled hot chocolate. I was going! I walked in the door. "Hello?" I said.
"Wait a minute," a mystery voice said. "Oh, I know who you are. Come out of the shadow, ho ho ho! Hello, Lena, I'm Santa. What are you doing here?"
"I fell through a magic door."
"Oh, hop on a reindeer, he will take you home."
"But wait, will I ever see you again?"
"Not if I can help it! Bye, Lena."
"Bye, Santa."

Ava Collie (9)
Portlethen Primary School, Portlethen

The Magic Door

I'm in my room. I see a magical door. I open it slowly. I see a football land. I decide to explore the football land. I meet Mo Salah and Kylian Mbappé. A robber steals the shining World Cup trophy! Me, Mo Salah, and Kylian Mbappé sprint after him. We manage to sprint as fast as a cheetah and catch him.

We all celebrate by inviting world-class footballers, like Pele and Neymar, to a party. In the VIP area, icons play football, eat, and drink. There also is a restaurant where you can get starters, mains, desserts, and drinks. There are massive mansions in Football Land where the pro footballers live.

The FIFA president gives me tickets to watch Brazil versus Croatia. Sadly, Croatia win 4-2 on penalties, so Brazil are out of the 2022 Qatar World Cup. I enjoyed watching, I did want Brazil to win though. I also get invited to the VIP area to play with the icon footballers and eat and drink.

Lyle Cruickshank (9)
Portlethen Primary School, Portlethen

The Magic Door

One day, I went upstairs to my room but the second I opened my door, I knew I was not in my room. I was somewhere cold. All I could see was snow. I started walking and, as I got closer, I started to see a wooden cabin. I went inside. It smelt like gingerbread.
As I walked around, I started to see lots of machines and I heard lots of little voices. I realised I was in Santa's workshop! I was so happy until the whole room went black! I didn't know what to do. I was scared, but I knew I had to do something.
I started to smell burning. One of the machines had stopped working and Santa did not know what to do. It was Christmas Eve tomorrow! So the elves and I got to work. First, we had to fix the lights, then we fixed the machine. We also checked the other machines, just in case.
Then, Santa was so happy. He gave me hot chocolate. Then, when I was done, I went back home and went to sleep.

Ruby Crossan (9)
Portlethen Primary School, Portlethen

The Magic Door

I opened the magic door in my school and found myself touching something really cold and wet. I walked in further. I smelt something like reindeer. Suddenly, I heard someone shouting, "Ho ho ho!" It sounded like Santa!
Quickly, I started running to a lit-up house in the distance. But the lights turned off. Suddenly, I got lost. I didn't know where to go. The moon came out. It was pitch-black. I heard something running toward me, it got closer and closer...
How surprised I was to see Santa! He said, "Come to the workshop, we will get you home by Christmas." I was so excited.
I jumped to my feet in excitement. "Yes, yes!" I shouted out loud, running to the workshop. I saw Rudolph, Dasher, and all the other reindeer. I saw elves and Mrs Claus. It was morning soon, so we went on Santa's sleigh and I got back in time for Christmas!

Amalie Watson (9)
Portlethen Primary School, Portlethen

Candy Land

Carefully, I opened the magic door and, as I walked through the magic door, I saw Candy Land! I saw lots of candy and lots of candyfloss. I smelt candyfloss.
But I walked too far and I couldn't find my way back. It was pitch-black, so I kept walking. I found a girl, she had rainbow eyes. She was also wearing a candyfloss dress and shoes.
I asked her for help and she politely said yes. Eventually, we found the creaky magic door.

Olivia Collie (9)
Portlethen Primary School, Portlethen

The Door To The Sea

"Don't forget to turn the lights off," reminded Sara's mum.
Sara was a little girl who loved swimming. Right now, she was just about to go to bed. She lay in bed with her teddy pressed against her soft pyjamas.
"Hey, you," a voice whispered next to Sara's head.
"Huh?" Sara was terrified! She looked next to her and saw her fox looking at her.
"Please help me get home," said the fox. It hopped out of the bed and went to the wall. "Take this chalk and draw a door." Sara drew a door and the fox jumped in.
Sara followed and they were in the ocean! A fox with blue antlers hugged the fox. "There you are!"
Sara was swimming in the cold ocean.
"Goodbye, Sara. Take this chalk and come visit me again and again!"
"Bye!" Sara jumped into the door and she was in her bedroom. "Amazing!"

Sara Esmaeli (8)
Quinton Church Primary School, Birmingham

The Magic Door

I once found a strange-looking key. It was used to open a magic door. I had to travel through this amazing door. I found an amazing world from the past. I wanted to explore this amazing, fun, and scary land.
It had animals of all different kinds. It also had treasure. But, best of all, it had amazing fairies flying over a dark scary river that once was all the colours of the rainbow. Some evil sorcerer had turned it black.
The strange key that opened the door was needed by the Fairy Queen to turn it all back to its amazing colours again. I had to run to find her, give her the key, and once she had it, she turned everything back to the beautiful colours it was.

Lauren Joyce (8)
Quinton Church Primary School, Birmingham

The Magical Fairy Garden

Once, there was a girl called Izzie and she saw this strange door in her house. She had never seen it before and it was pink and sparkly. After a few hours, she decided to go and open the door.
When she opened the door, she saw a nice garden so she decided to explore the garden. Then she saw fairy sparkles. She was interested, so she kept walking. Then she saw fairies and the fairies saw Izzie. They showed her around.
Izzie felt so happy and excited because she played with the fairies.

Zoe Curwood (9)
Quinton Church Primary School, Birmingham

Mysterious Forest

Once, I heard sounds coming from the wardrobe. I opened it and was surprised, in front of me was a green forest! Me and my toy rabbit went to explore it. My rabbit toy came alive!
The forest was amazing, green trees, colourful flowers. Going through the forest was a beautiful river. Birds and butterflies flew around. We met forest fairies! The fairies took us flying and showed us around. That was amazing.
We flew through the forest. We saw so many birds and butterflies. There were so many sounds around. We saw the blue ocean and dolphins spoke to us. There were so many beautiful flowers with a beautiful smell. We met lots of animals.
We had tea and cake in the fairies' house. We had an amazing time. And then I woke up! My toy rabbit was in my hand. I went to my wardrobe and there was nothing inside.

Laila Ghannam Begdouri (6)
Springfield Primary School, Sunbury-On-Thames

Jake And The Magic Door

One sunny morning, Jake was walking down Clock Rd when, suddenly, he saw an old, abandoned door. When he opened the door, without warning, someone behind Jake elbowed him through the door. When Jake woke up, he could see shiny, glistening dragons gliding and flying through the clouds.

Amazed, Jake timidly approached a nearby dragon. All of a sudden, the terrific dragon span around and shot Jake into the freezing cold atmosphere. When Jake landed on the ground, he saw a sign saying: *Don't touch the ground if you want to feel down*. Jake wandered further into this peculiar world.

When he got to a fresh lake, Jake stopped to wash his face. A hand forced him to the dry, green ground. All at once, Jake remembered what he had been told. Instantly, he dived into the water. When he looked back, he could see sharks. Jake grasped a shell and his whole life flashed before his eyes. When he woke up, he found himself home. When he got home, two very strange things happened: firstly, he found the shell in his pocket and secondly, he never saw the door again.

Athulan Uthayakumar (9)
The Coppice Primary School, Hollywood

The Mimi Doll

An extract

Sofie is ten. One day, she hears a crash in her room. She dashes upstairs to see what has happened. Sofie's favourite doll, Mimi, has moved! Sofie puts the doll back and goes to eat her dinner. She is told that she can read in bed, so she does. Sofie just settles down when she realises that her doll is pointing at something on the wall, and then goes through it. Sofie is in shock! She follows the doll. Suddenly, she is in Toy Land where toys are alive!

"Someone is on the loose! I think she's called Iris. She put the place on self-destruct mode! I need help to stop Iris!" Mimi says dramatically.

"What is this place?" asks Sofie.

"It's a land filled with teddies, dolls like me, figures, singing toys, and model dolls! We call it Toy Land for short," says Mimi. "But anyway, I need your help!" Mimi says in despair.

"Okay!" Sofie says. "I'll help." She picks up a small device. "What's this?"

"Oh, that's what set the whole place on a timer to self-destruct!" says Mimi.

"I'll just destroy it then," Sofie says.
Behind Mimi comes a thundering laugh. Mimi knows that sound well: Iris. "Give that device to me. Toy Land is over!"
Sofie looks at Iris, she has her face in a grimace.
"Why do you want to destroy Toy Land?" Sofie asks calmly.
"No one ever bought me any toys. Said I didn't deserve them. Said I was too rough."

Beau B (8)
The Coppice Primary School, Hollywood

The Magic Door

Zora had always been a daydreamer. One sunny day, Zora was writing a poem about dragons when she went into one of her daydreams. In this daydream, Zora saw a huge door in front of her. She was curious as to what was behind the door, so she moved closer.

Suddenly, the door swung open and Zora was sucked inside. All Zora could see for miles was vast darkness. She slowly crept forward when, suddenly, she heard mumbling, screeching, and bubbling. Zora kept going toward the sound.

She peered inside a cave and saw what was making the noise she'd heard. The things that were making the noises were creatures being tormented by a soul-sucking demon! There were trolls mumbling, lava dragons covering a hot bubbling lava pool, and a crystal dragon screeching as she tried to protect her diamond eggs.

Zora could feel the pain of the tormented creatures and wanted to try and save them from their torment. She moved toward the demon and threw a rock to distract him. The creatures saw this as a chance to try and escape. In the blink of an eye, Zora picked up a diamond egg and ran for her life with the creatures following her. The demon chased after her.

"Zora, Zora wake up!" Zora woke up, feeling the hot breath of her teacher on her face. *Oh no,* Zora thought, *I'm going to be in so much trouble!* Her frustrated teacher said, "Daydreaming again, Zora?"

Zayyan Miah (9)
The Coppice Primary School, Hollywood

The Secret Door Of Mythical Creatures

One sunny morning, there was a girl called Natalie. One morning, she was watching TV when, suddenly, she heard whispers. She went into her kitchen to see what it was. She could see that there was a random wooden door glowing.
She opened the door and saw nothing, except for complete darkness. All of a sudden, something grabbed her and pulled her in. When she reached the ground, she could see golden eggs, glowing crystals, and beautiful creatures flying in the air. By a cave, there was a sign that said: *If you start to wonder, you will hear a roar of thunder!* Natalie shuddered and walked away. Unfortunately, Natalie started to wonder how this land got there. Suddenly, she remembered what she had been told. Just then, she heard a big roar of thunder! It was a dragon!
As quick as flash, she started to sprint away. Luckily, she saw the door that she had come through, so she hopped in.

When she reached home, two very strange things happened: first, nobody knew that the door was there; secondly, she never saw the door again. Had it disappeared or could she not see it? She would never know.

Florence Troth (9)
The Coppice Primary School, Hollywood

Vicki And The Horrendous Halloween Night

"Argh!" I screamed.
Wait a second, let's rewind this story to the start.
I'm Vicki Foster and I'm the most curious girl in the world. It was a pitch-black night and I was searching for some batteries for my torch, up in the attic. Suddenly, I saw a glimpse of what seemed to be a door knob.
I dragged my eyes back to it. It was an orange door with a yellow knob. As I said before, I'm the most curious girl in the world, so, with much trepidation, I opened it. I screamed.
I was standing there, open-mouthed, in shock, staring at something that looked like a tropical island. It was full to the brim with cabins, each representing something that I thought were supposed to be Greek gods. That's when it hit me - I was the daughter of a Greek god!
Finally, after what seemed like hours, I woke up. Back in my room. I didn't remember falling asleep. All I can be 100% sure of is, that night was the most horrendous Halloween ever!

Ellie Dunn (8)
The Coppice Primary School, Hollywood

The Magic Room

There once was a boy named Peter. He lived with his little sister, Millie, and his mum and dad. One day, he and his sister were outside when their mum and dad called them in. They came to find dinner on the table. They sat down and started to eat. Suddenly, Dad said, "You can say it."

"Okay!" Mum said. "We're moving house!"

"Oh!" Peter said, shocked.

"We're moving tomorrow, so pack your bags," Mum said.

They packed their bags and set off. When they got there, Peter headed straight for the basement. The door creaked open and he stepped inside. It was a tiny room and it had loads of pictures with spiderwebs on them.

Just then, somebody called his name. It echoed around the room. Then, loads of the pictures moved and there was a door. Peter ran out of the basement. He woke up, realising it was a dream, and went back to sleep!

Erica Watkins (8)

The Coppice Primary School, Hollywood

The Magic Door

Once upon a time, there was a girl named Megan. Every day, she would walk down a bendy path. One day, she saw a magical door that she had never seen before.
Quickly, Megan opened the door. Inside it was pitch-black. The first thing Megan saw was a long and mysterious path covered by long, green grass. Then she saw her friend's house, maybe she was there too.
When she walked in, she didn't see her friend, she saw something way cooler. Inside, there were posh tables and some strange people talking. There were people serving fresh potatoes, steaming apple pies and yummy ice cream, with hot chocolate covered with marshmallows and whipped cream.
Then Megan noticed that all the people were staring at her. They looked so fierce that Megan ran as quick as a flash, all the way back home. Luckily, Megan got home and lived happily ever after.

Megan Millard (9)
The Coppice Primary School, Hollywood

The Magic Acorn

One sunny, hot day, a pretty girl called Jade wandered into the big street. Suddenly, she saw a massive, amazing, dark hole in the middle of the pavement. To her amazement, she tripped over an old brown log and fell in.
Inside, she could see a scary abandoned house with rats running across the creaky floorboards. All she could hear was ghosts mumbling, and all she could feel was the creepy old stairs. After ten minutes, she started to feel lonely and scared. "How am I going to get out of this place?" asked Jade. Suddenly, she saw a sparkling blue light by the staircase! It was a magic acorn! Quickly, she picked it up and wished. Then, *poof!* She was back in the big street. Once she was home, she started to think about how scary her day was. But maybe it was all a dream.

Eva Elwell (9)
The Coppice Primary School, Hollywood

The Magic Door

One school day, Caitlyn was walking home from school. Just then, she realised no one was in the church. Sneakily, she tiptoed toward the church door. She knocked on the door and walked in. She looked around and saw colourful bees, multicoloured butterflies, and children planting seeds. She heard bees buzzing and children laughing. Caitlyn felt soft and squishy pollen. She saw a sign that read: *Don't pick a flower, or lose your power.*
Caitlyn wandered further into the farm. In the middle of a field, she saw a golden poppy. She picked it, then gasped. She had been warned about this! Suddenly, she heard millions of shrieks. Eagerly, she ran to the portal and went through it. She was safe.

Emily A (8)
The Coppice Primary School, Hollywood

The Magic Door

Once upon a time, there were two girls called Violet and Felicity. They went to the front door but it didn't lead them outside, it took them to the past!
When they went through the door, they saw a dinosaur! They were terrified! But it wasn't mean, it was kind. The dinosaur had hurt its leg so the girls looked in their bags and gave the dinosaur a bandage and the dinosaur was back to normal. The dinosaur didn't have anything to thank them with, so the dinosaur gave them one of her baby dinosaurs. After that, the girls went back through the door and it took them home.

Daisy Watkins (8)
The Coppice Primary School, Hollywood

What Is It Like Down There?

Hello, I'm Isaac. I want you to meet my friends, Theo, Blake, Isla, and Maeve. Now I'll tell you what happened.
When we were playing hide-and-seek, I found a bush. It looked like a cloud in a tree shape so, like a normal person, you would try to avoid the weird-looking bush. But I was a weirdo so I went in there. There was really tall grass. There was wet soil under my feet. It was leaking through my shoes. I ran through the grass but then there was a ringing sound and I woke up! Was it real or not? But my feet were wet!

Isaac Mason (9)
The Coppice Primary School, Hollywood

The Magic Door

Once upon a time, I was ready for school. But when I opened my front door, I saw a snow-covered land! Then I heard a beautiful sound. I went exploring to find out who made the sound.
I skipped through the snow into a frozen forest. The sun was warm and shining, sparkles of frost covered the branches. I came across a boy called George Burrows. His skin was covered in soft brown fur. George said, "Hello, Skye, what are you doing here?"
I told him I was exploring to find who made that amazing song. George asked what it sounded like. I told him it sounded like, *tweet-tweet, twoo-twoo-twoo!* He said he knew who it was, it was his friend Twooloo the bluebird. She had got lost! I told George I could help find his friend.

Skye H Albers (7)
Warlingham Park School, Chelsham Common

Rosie And The Magic Door

Once upon a time, there was a girl called Rosie. She loved Christmas. On a cloudy Sunday afternoon, while she was making hot chocolate for her family as they finished the last Christmas decorations, her dog, Buster, was growling at a kitchen cupboard.
When she went to check it out, Rosie saw a pink and blue swirling portal waiting for her. Before Rosie could do anything, she got sucked in and landed on her bottom in a pile of snow! A pack of baby huskies ran up to her from a village named, Santa's Village.
Rosie loved huskies so much that when they ran back to the village, she ran after them. When she walked into the small town, there were rainbow elves and fairies everywhere. It was like a lost treasure chest. This was her dream town. She made friends and made snow angels and snowmen with all her elf and fairy friends.

After playing for a while, Rosie decided that it was time to go home. She found the portal and jumped through it. When she got home, it was bedtime. Rosie rushed to bed to wait for Santa to visit her house.

Rosie Murphy (6)
Warlingham Park School, Chelsham Common

Rainbow Snow

Once upon a time, Rose was in Mexico and it was one more week until Christmas. Rose was getting bored, then she saw a wormhole that was like a magic door! It took her to the north pole. She saw Santa and she said, "I must be dreaming!" She couldn't feel anything as she was so cold.
"You are not dreaming, Rose. You are in Santa's village and I need you to save Christmas!" said Santa.
"But Santa, it doesn't matter what gifts people have, it's who they are with at Christmastime."
Santa thought for a moment and then he realised Rose was right. All he needed to do was make sure that there was love in the north pole and in the world. Later, rainbow snow came down from the sky.

Chloe Cruz Roque (6)
Warlingham Park School, Chelsham Common

The Magic Door To Snow Land

Once upon a time, Tapi was asleep on a hot afternoon until a portal appeared. It led to the magic door. Tapi opened the door and saw trees rustling, and found people and animals frozen. It was horrifying and terrifying!
Then Tapi saw white snow on the ground. Tapi could feel the cold white snow covering the land. The witch came out of a haunted house. The witch had cast a strange, evil spell and the people were sad. It was scary.
The witch was happy casting her spells. The witch saw Tapi as she was throwing ice cubes at people. She tried to throw some at Tapi. Tapi ran back to the magical door as the witch gave chase. She was angry because she wanted to freeze Tapi but Tapi escaped.

Tapiwanashe Shambira (6)
Warlingham Park School, Chelsham Common

The Secret City

On a warm, sunny afternoon, I stepped into my conservatory. A door made of sparkling gold, chiselled quartz, and cobbled stone appeared before me. I opened the door and ran in, curious to explore.
I found myself on an island in the sky. It was a city made of beautiful iron and fabulous gold. I looked around and found an iron trapdoor. I went down some stairs, then I saw all of my friends! We played in the castle, temple, basement, downstairs, upstairs, the mezzanine, and the balcony. We had so much fun, then we got tired and hungry.
We all went through the same door and ended up in my house. We all had a sleepover and their parents collected them the next day.

Isaac Payne (6)
Warlingham Park School, Chelsham Common

The Quantum Realm

It was a normal day and I was watching TV. All of a sudden, the TV went black and started to glow bright yellow. It was sending sparks all over the room and eventually, it stopped but the bright yellow glow of the door was still there.
My natural instinct would tell me not to go through, but I was so curious and just couldn't help myself. The second I stepped through, I could feel myself falling into doom. "*Ahh!*" I cried as I fell down. *Splash!* Eventually, I reached the floor - but it wasn't the floor, it was water which meant I survived.
There were floating rocks in yellow, green and red. They went on for infinity upwards and were constantly crashing. Without warning, a huge rock came flying towards me and... it was all a dream.

Toby Cooper (11)
Werrington Community Primary School, Yeolmbridge

The Cinna-Monster Magic Cauldron

Marcus, a ten-year-old kid, knows a little bit about magic. A bathtub full of cinnamon, a pot full of glue and rocks, a squeeze of dry ice, and a spoonful of ink. *Crash! Ding!* The cinna-monster has been awakened.
There is havoc on the streets and the biggest monster on Earth. "It's taking over Aroma City," shouts one woman.
"Argh!" screams a man.
"Don't worry," say the police. "We've got this."
They pull out a giant tub of water and then suddenly, "Argh!" the cinna-monster screams as he disappears
"Woohoo!" shouts everyone citizen from Aroma City.

Marcus Langton (10)
Werrington Community Primary School, Yeolmbridge

Dog World

One day there was a lost puppy called Rex (he was small and funny). He never left his mum because people try to kick him or try to run him over. Then someone adopted them in a cosy lovely cottage with a dog bed (for his mum to give birth to puppies) and owners called Paige and Mark. They were mad about dogs.
After Rex went outside he fell down a hole. He barked as loudly as he could but they locked the door and forgot Rex was outside. They finally got him out and went to bed.
Then Rex's dog mum, Daisy, gave birth to 10 babies. They were shocked. After the puppies were named Rex felt left out. Rex ran out but they became a happy family.

Esmae Keane Aldridge (9)
Werrington Community Primary School, Yeolmbridge

Under The Sea

One day, a girl called Alya was walking to the park when she saw a door. "A door?" she said, scared. Then she opened the door and fell in. "*Ahh!*" she screamed.
"Hi, I'm Chloe," said a mermaid. "You can breathe," she said.
"Thanks for telling me," Alya replied. "Can you take me back to the door?" Alya asked.
"Sure," said Chloe. Then Chloe placed her hand on Alya and pulled her to the door.
"Bye!" they both shouted.

Willow Hunter (8)
Werrington Community Primary School, Yeolmbridge

Tokyo, Japan

Once upon a time, a man was in the forest. He found a mysterious door and he smirked and went through it to Tokyo in Japan. He heard gunshots getting fired, flies flying and caterpillars crawling. He was horrified.

He jumped into a room full of statues. One moved, he almost had a heart attack. He ran so fast to the door that he went through. In the blink of an eye, it was gone. He grinned and moaned.

He felt like he was in a dream. He ran into the statues' room and hoped there was another door there...

Robert Swiderski (9)
Werrington Community Primary School, Yeolmbridge

Ohio

One day, in the UK, I was in the middle of nowhere but there was a mischievous door. I was like, *Would this take me anywhere?* Then I opened the door.
Inside was black, white, crazy, so I jumped in. There I was in Ohio, some crazy place. "Now I'm here," I said loudly. Then I saw a dog. I saw an upside-down car. I saw a banana eating a monkey.
Then I was ready to leave. Someone said bye then I said bye too.

Charlie Smith (9)
Werrington Community Primary School, Yeolmbridge

Horse Land

In Horse Land, horses galloped in the fields. Then a wild horse came to see what was going on in Horse Land. Then a bunch of people came to see what was going on.

The wild horse ran away until people got their horses and chased the horse. The horse hid behind a tree. The people galloped past the horse. The horse galloped deep into the woods. The horse went to Horse Land.

Imogen Wingard (8)
Werrington Community Primary School, Yeolmbridge

We hope you have enjoyed reading this book – and that you will continue to in the coming years.

If you're the parent or family member of an enthusiastic poet or story writer, do visit our website **www.youngwriters.co.uk/subscribe** and sign up to receive news, competitions, writing challenges and tips, activities and much, much more! There's lots to keep budding writers motivated!

If you would like to order further copies of this book, or any of our other titles, then please give us a call or order via your online account.

Young Writers
Remus House
Coltsfoot Drive
Peterborough
PE2 9BF
(01733) 890066
info@youngwriters.co.uk

Join in the conversation!
Tips, news, giveaways and much more!

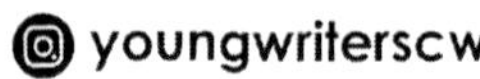